Ambassadors of Thought World

A Tale of Infinity and Imagination

by
Penyu Tortue

Book Industry Study Group (BISAC) subject:
visionary and metaphysical fiction
FIC039000

paper ISBN: 979-8-9940069-0-0

hardbound ISBN: 979-8-9940069-1-7

eISBN: 979-8-9940069-2-4

Dedicated to everyone who has ever tried to comprehend infinity.

Prelude

I am a very old turtle. My name is Penyu Tortue, and I have a story to tell. Since I have the brain and body of an old turtle, I cannot write or speak. I had to find a volunteer to help me communicate my message. So I sent out a call in thought world to recruit an ambassador to relate my story about infinity and imagination. I was overwhelmed by the response. I decided to choose more than one ambassador, as I believe multiple perspectives are valuable.

The ambassadors were extraordinarily lucky to connect with a real person right away. Not only that, they had the uncommonly good fortune to find someone gullible enough to believe my story on the very first try. Truly incredible. The spider web must have worked.

1.
Open

Nature called, and I awoke. I sat up on my cot and retrieved my glasses from a tent pocket. I pulled on my shoes, unzipped the tent door and stepped out into the forest. The night air was perfect for camping. Pleasant temperature, dry air, just a slight breeze. A waxing gibbous moon was high above. Despite being in a mature forest under a dense canopy of leaves, dappled moonlight allowed me to see all right without a flashlight.

To my surprise, the light of an unusually white campfire shone about half a football field away. I stepped to the dark side of a large tree to do my business. A real advantage of out of the way campsites is the privacy. On my way back to my tent, I looked toward the flickering white light. The campfire was where I had been sitting earlier. Sometimes the best spot for my tent is not the best place to sit and enjoy the woods. The campfire was in a very pretty location among the trees. I had sat over there through sunset to relax, think, and observe the life surrounding me.

Two people sitting by the campfire waved to me

and enthusiastically motioned for me to come over. Funny, I did not remember seeing or hearing anyone else camping nearby. They must have arrived after I had gone to bed. They motioned me over again. Perhaps they needed something.

I grabbed three bottles of water and walked over. A man and a woman were illuminated by their firelight. The woman once again waved for me to come over, as if to encourage me from changing my mind about meeting them. They seemed to relax as I made my way among the trees.

Just before I reached their camp site, I caught a spider web square in the face. "Blech!" I balanced the water bottles in one arm and frantically swept my face with the sleeve of my other arm. "Yuck!" I swept my face with my free hand.

"Don't move!" cried out the man.

"Please, please hold perfectly still," implored the woman.

Both were looking intently at my hand. I looked down and saw a large bioluminescent spider glowing on my thumb.

"Please don't move," repeated the man.

"Is it harmful?" I asked.

"Only if you cause it fear or anger," the woman explained. "Then its glow could severely burn you. Tim, can you take care of it?"

"Yes, Amy." Tim looked directly into my eyes. Tim had kind eyes. "What is your name?"

"Steve."

"Steve, please hold perfectly still and I will take care of it," Tim said as he walked quietly toward me.

The spider was unlike any I had ever seen. It had a rectangular body that glowed in pulses of blue, green, red and yellow light. Its eight legs were curved in a gentle cup. It looked for all the world to me like a tiny screen with a dish antenna attached to its back. Tim quietly extended his hand, palm up, until his middle finger almost touched my thumb. The spider jumped onto Tim's hand and scurried up his sleeve. I expected Tim to jerk or shake his arm, but instead he quietly returned to his camp chair.

Steve: Doesn't that feel creepy?

Tim: No, it will be safe now.

Amy: Please have a seat, Steve.

Tim: We are ever so glad you thought to join us, Steve.

That spider was so weird. I felt a bit rattled and unsure how to respond.

Steve: Uh, would you like a bottle of water?

Tim: No, thank you. Please have a seat.

Amy: No, but thank you for offering. We do wish you would sit with us.

A third chair was positioned opposite the campfire from where Tim and Amy sat. I placed the water bottles under the chair and sat down. For a camp chair it was surprisingly comfortable. But I had a weird sensation like a spider web was wrapped around my head.

Amy: We have been hoping to gain your attention for some time now, so your company is most welcome.

Steve, combing my fingers through my hair: This is a remarkably comfortable chair.

Amy: We are so glad you like it.

Steve: So why do you want to meet with me?

Tim: To talk.

Steve: That's all, just talk?

Amy: Yes, talk to convey some ideas and get your feedback.

Tim: We have a project to complete.

Amy: And we need your participation.

Tim: In fact, your participation in our project is vital to us.

I looked around Amy and Tim's campsite. All I could see were the three of us, our chairs, and the campfire. No vehicle. No tent. Very odd. I rubbed my face. I mean, I personally enjoy camping in remote areas of the forest. I have my car and big tent and the usual camping gear. But these two seemed to be out here with nothing but a few chairs. Their tent must be pitched somewhere nearby out of sight.

Steve: What kind of project?

Tim: We are Ambassadors of Thought World, beckoned here to meet with you.

Amy: Our project is to tell you a story from thought world and get your reactions.

Ambassadors of Thought World. That's a new one. I could not help but wonder what they were really up to. I mussed my hair with my fingers. Perhaps they were going to try to sell me something? Or they were missionaries of some sort? They both seemed friendly and kind, so I was not afraid of them harming me in any way.

Steve: Ambassadors of Thought World? Is that near Schenectady?

Tim: No, thought world is not tied to any one location.

Steve: Who beckoned you?

Amy: Penyu Tortue.

Steve: Wait, sorry, but before we go on, there is something I just have to ask you. Why is the campfire white?

Tim and Amy tensed up and exchanged a nervous glance. They looked a little panicked.

Amy: Um, why do you ask?

Steve: Well usually the flames are mostly yellow, and close to the burning wood the flames are orange or red.

Especially hot fires might have some blue flames. But I have never seen a campfire that is all white like that.

I was meeting Amy's eyes as I spoke. When I looked back at the fire the flames were yellow, and the embers were red.

Steve: Hey, how did you do that?

Tim: Do what?

Steve: Make the fire look normal all of a sudden like that.

Amy: We didn't do anything.

Why were they gaslighting me? And how did they create that illusion?

Steve: Then what made the fire change?

Tim: May we explain later? We could try now, but it will all make a lot more sense if you let us first explain our project.

That campfire illusion made me very curious as to just who Tim and Amy really were and what they were up to. That spider was weird. But Tim had no problem with it scrambling up his sleeve. Ambassadors of Thought World. Sounds like the name of a chess team. The two of them seemed sincere and benign. Well, except that Amy was an impressively solidly built woman. If her sport was track, her primary event definitely looked to be shot put. Maybe she was a powerlifter. Perhaps even a rugby player. Tim was very slightly built. Not unhealthy, but small and thin. Tim's sport looked to be chess or online gaming. Maybe if his testosterone was raging he'd go for a round of disc golf. They were an odd couple, so physically different from one another. It seemed to me that if Amy had a mind to, she could pick Tim right up and break him in two like a dry twig.

Steve: So I am supposed to believe that you are Ambassadors of Thought World, and all I have to do is listen to what you have to say and then tell you what I think?

Amy: That's right.

Steve: And me doing this is vital to your project.

Tim: Correct.

Steve: Who is Penyu Tortue?

Amy: Giver of our instructions as Ambassadors of Thought World.

I silently rubbed my cheeks as I thought about how to respond. This encounter was unusual in so many ways even beyond the whole Ambassadors of Thought World act. Tim and Amy were way out here next to my remote campsite with no apparent means of transportation and provided me with a crazy comfortable chair next to a trick fire. Who *are* these two calling themselves Ambassadors of Thought World? It occurred to me that the university was fairly close by. Maybe Amy and Tim were graduate students in psychology or anthropology doing some kind of study. This whole Ambassadors of

Thought World routine could be the treatment phase of an experiment. They might be investigating how people who like remote camping react to "Ambassadors of Thought World." Such a project would be more than a little bit weird, but stranger projects are undertaken in academia all the time. I decided to play along. If for no other reason, I wanted to find out at the end how they made a campfire look pure white.

Steve: Okay, I'll cooperate.

Tim, surprised: Really? You really will?

Tim bounced up and down in his chair as he spoke. Amy massaged her temples with her fingertips as Tim gushed with excitement.

Tim: I mean really that is really good. Most excellent, even. That you will cooperate. We are really so happy you will join us. We're so delighted you like your chair. We are very happy you are choosing to cooperate with our project.

Amy: Tim!

Tim stopped bouncing and pushed his thick glasses up into the bridge of his nose. Amy glared at Tim. Tim stuck his tongue out at Amy. Amy gave Tim the hairy eyeball. Then she turned to me and smiled. Amy had a big, friendly smile.

Steve: So do you have the required informed consent form for me to sign?

Tim and Amy both gave me the same deer in the headlights look as when I asked why the fire was white. Amy shifted uncomfortably in her chair. Tim wrung his hands together, then pushed his glasses up the bridge of his nose again. I combed my hair with my fingers.

Amy: Did you forget the form, Tim?

Tim: What form?

Amy, hissing between her teeth: The ingrown intent form Steve here is talking about. The one you forgot.

Amy jutted her chin out at Tim and raised both eyebrows high as she spoke.

Tim: Oh, yeah, the deformed content form. Right. Yes. Sorry. I did kind of forget it. Really sorry about that. I did not mean to forget it. The form I mean. I really did not mean to forget the form.

Amy, snarling: Enough, Tim.

Amy looked ready to bite Tim's head off in one chomp. It was strange enough that they did not have the form. Stranger still was how two graduate students could not know what an informed consent form was. It made no sense at all. Maybe they did know, but pretended not to. Fake ignorance might be part of the treatment phase of this "Ambassadors of Thought World" experiment. By now I was so curious about where this was all headed I chose to defuse the situation.

Steve: Never mind, the informed consent form is not

that big of a deal. We can figure it all out in the end. But please explain to me again just what it is I am agreeing to cooperate with.

Amy: Our project is to share Penyu Tortue's story.

Steve: Who's Penyu Tortue again?

Amy: He sent us here.

Steve: From where?

Tim: Thought world.

Steve, snickering: Oh, right, you two are Ambassadors of Thought World. I almost forgot.

Tim: After our presentation in two parts, you will decide what you think.

Steve: What are the two parts?

Tim: Being and knowing.

Steve: Just what do you mean by "you will decide what you think?" That is all there is to it? Will there be a test?

Amy: Yes, that is all there is to it.

Tim: No test. Well at least not any formal kind of test. I guess you could say we'll be testing your credulity.

Amy gave Tim an I-am-going-to-snap-you-in-two look and silently mouthed that she could punch Tim so hard his nose was going to poke out the back side of his head.

Steve: So I can decide you are both full of hooey and reject what you present, and there will be no reward or penalty?

Amy: That is correct.

Steve: So what is in it for you?

Tim, rubbing the back of his head: Everything, actually.

Steve: You are saying this Ambassadors of Thought World routine is practically a life or death thing.

Amy: Practically. If you do not listen and pay attention and respond, our project fails.

Tim: And our project means everything to us.

They seemed to be exaggerating the importance of my participation in their study. It struck me as an exaggeration, anyway. I could not understand how my cooperation with their project could be that vital to their existence. But their graduate degrees could well depend on completing their research project. Maybe they needed one last set of data that happened to be me. So I could understand why they were so earnest.

Steve: Okay, I will listen, pay attention, and respond. Can I ask questions as we go?

Tim: Yes, of course. In fact we would be very surprised if you will not have questions. And we will have questions for you.

Steve: Fair enough.

Amy: There is one essential thing to emphasize. You must tell us the truth to the best of your ability. If you say anything that is not true, from that moment forward you will not know whether what we tell you is true or not. If you are truthful with us, we will be truthful to you.

Steve: I have never read honesty worded quite that way on any informed consent form. Good idea, though. What if I make a mistake, and accidentally say something false?

Tim: Unfortunately, it is still the case that from that point forward you will not know whether what we tell you is true or not.

Steve: That's kind of harsh.

Amy: It is, but we don't create the rule. It's just the way things are.

Tim: If you inject dissonance, you disrupt harmony.

Amy: If you tell a lie, the lie echoes.

Steve: Do I have to take a pledge or sign something?

Tim: It doesn't matter. You are either truthful or not, regardless of your intentions up front.

Amy: But a pledge is not a bad idea. You know, Tim, a ritual fits with our project, and doing a ritual does match Steve's culture.

They must be anthropology students.

Tim: Very well. Steve, repeat after me, "I pledge to tell the truth to the best of my ability."

Steve: Wait, shouldn't I pledge to always tell the truth, without the "best of my ability" part?

Tim: Well, given that you are one finite living organism, however much you try to always tell the truth, you can never know for certain that you are correct. So that pledge would be beyond what you can really commit to.

I vigorously rubbed my face. Finite living organism? What the heck? Just play along.

Steve: Fair enough. I pledge to tell the truth to the best of my ability.

Tim: Good. Now let's start our project.

Interlude One

Before we continue with Amy and Tim's project, I need to explain two things. First, I am the amanuensis writing Penyu Tortue's story. No, "amanuseance" (if that is how it is spelled, I seem to have a mental block about the correct spelling) does not mean "I'm a nuisance," even though that is what it sounds like. Amanunsis is a fancy, old fashioned word meaning someone who writes down a story on behalf of another. In this case, Penyu Tortue was not only unable to write for himself, he was also unable to speak. He has the brain and body of an old turtle, after all. So the only way for Penyu to communicate his message was for me to be a character in his story. You see, the character Steve is the conscious being who wrote Penyu's story down so you can read it. Penyu Tortue dearly wants people to read his story. So here I wrote it down. So you can read it.

The second thing I need to explain before we go on is my excuse for being so gullible. Throughout this experience, I felt fine when I stayed focused on Amy, Tim, the characters we met, and the experiences we had. I felt great, in fact. But the moment my mind wandered, it felt like a spider web was plastered to my whole head. Which was very uncomfortable. So I tried to avoid that. I learned that if I stayed focused on my immediate environment, I felt fine. It worked really well for me to pay attention and think in the moment. I played along because the ride felt wonderful, which from your perspective may seem rather gullible or even dumb. Nevertheless, you may find it rewarding to play along and enjoy the ride in thought world, too. Just saying.

Now on with Penyu Tortue's story. We were about to start Tim and Amy's project about what it means to be.

2.
Be

Tim: We shall start with a few basic ideas. Some ideas cannot be picked apart or explained based on other more basic ideas. First, infinity is.

Amy: Steve, do you believe infinity is?

Steve: Sure. It seems simple enough that infinity is.

Tim: Yes, it seems simple. But accepting that infinity is has profound implications.

Amy: We mean it actually is.

Tim: Infinity is not just a concept in math or an idea in peoples' minds.

Steve: I'm okay with that.

Amy: That was way too easy.

Tim: Are you sure, Steve, that infinity is?

Steve: Yes.

Tim shifted in his chair and pushed his thick glasses up into the bridge of his nose. He looked perplexed and unhappy.

Amy: Let us move on, Tim. We can come back later to how infinity is.

Tim, reluctantly: Okay. The next basic idea is that infinity is waves.

Amy: It's all infinite waves. Everything. Infinite waves.

Steve: What kind of waves?

Amy: Every imaginable kind of wave: actual, potential, virtual, theoretical. Solid things are made of standing waves so tiny they cannot be seen. But the waves are there inside things. Everything is waves.

Tim: It's all infinite waves.

Amy: Infinite waves are everything.

Tim: You exist in a field of infinite waves.

Steve: Is repeating the same idea an example of the infinite waves?

Amy: Yes.

Tim: Everything is ultimately made of waves. Like Amy said, at your scale the stable resonances of tiny waves make solid things.

Amy: Relations among things are always by means of waves. That includes the resonances among electrons, protons, and neutrons that make up atoms. The atoms then resonate with one another to make the stuff you experience in the real world.

Tim: Which means every thing, and every relationship within every thing, no matter how small or how large, is caused by resonances within the infinite waves.

Steve: So how did all the waves and things get here in the first place?

Tim: You mean, why is there something rather than nothing?

Steve: Yes. That is the big unknown, right? I mean, we would all like to know how something came from nothing. You know, why beings like us exist at all. To put it in your way, why all the infinite waves exist, and why resonances in the infinite waves create things. Can you answer that?

Tim: We will do our best. As Ambassadors of Thought World, we are here to share Penyu Tortue's story about how infinity chooses to be. So we are now going to read you a creation myth.

Amy: Our creation myth is a story of how infinity creates something from nothing, and how infinity includes beings.

Amanuscianse: Creation myth! Amy and Tim must be graduate students in anthropology doing a study on how people react to a creation myth. I wondered which myth they would tell me. There are plenty to choose from. I have always gotten a kick out of that mud on the back of a turtle story.

Amy: Tim, why don't you do the honors.

Tim: No. You have such a nice voice, Amy. You read the creation myth to Steve.

Amy placed one hand into her lap with her palm facing up. She moved the fingers on her free hand in a motion to enlarge an image on a screen. A tablet appeared in her palm. Amy then moved her hands as if to open a book. The tablet magically expanded and unfolded to become a book.

Imanusciance: The fluorescence of a book out of one's palms was a really slick magic trick. The book trick was at least as slick as the campfire trick. I had become even more curious about the experimental treatment Amy and Tim were going to give me for their research project. If they performed such convincing illusions, they must have interesting things to tell me. I figured I could ask about the magic tricks once we were done with this whole Ambassadors of Thought World routine.

Amy cleared her throat and read:

How Infinity Created Being.

When the infinite one awoke, infinite waves came to be. The waves came from boundless unity, boundless order, and boundless chaos. Infinity was perfect. All was one.

Infinity thought that while perfection was good, there seemed to be something missing. There was never anything new, no change, no life. What is needed are beings. But how shall beings come to exist?

Tim was silently mouthing the words as Amy spoke.

The infinite one considered how beings might exist. Infinity has three natures: unity, order, and chaos. Infinity's natures are attracted to each other. But unity, order and chaos are always distinct. Attraction and distinction cause infinite waves. The infinite waves of unity, order, and chaos interact and may resonate.

When unity resonates with order, there are idea waves.

When order resonates with chaos, there are stuff waves.

The infinite one thought about how unity, order, and chaos resonate with idea and stuff. But still there were no beings. There were no beings because the stuff waves and the idea waves were propagating at infinity. All was one.

Beings are resonances of idea and stuff. Beings can only exist in time and space. So the infinite one creates time and space by limiting how fast stuff waves and idea waves can propagate. Stuff waves propagate at the speed of light. Idea waves propagate at inflation. Resonances of idea waves and stuff waves in time and space create pulses of being.

Each pulse of being is a harmonic resonance of unity, order, chaos, idea and stuff.

Beings are why there is something and not nothing.

All beings, including you, are unique resonances of unity, order, chaos, idea and stuff.

Amy closed the book, and moved the fingers of one hand so that the book shrank back down and disappeared up her sleeve.

Tim: You see, Steve, you and everything you can perceive exists as harmonic resonances of the infinite waves.

Amy: A being is a resonance of unity, order, chaos, idea, and stuff.

Tim: When the infinite one limits the propagation of idea waves and stuff waves, resonances of the waves create pulses of being.

Amy: The beauty and elegance of creation is awe inspiring.

Tim: It is amazing how infinity's three natures and limits on the propagation of idea and stuff create our infinitely complex pulse of being.

Amy: The elegant beauty of existence is awesome. There is something rather than nothing because unity, order, chaos, idea and stuff harmonize.

Tim, enraptured: Creation is all just so beautiful.

Amy: Except for slugs. Slugs are just gross.

Steve: I have never heard that creation myth. It's interesting. So you are saying that being is due to a five-way resonance?

Tim: Yes.

Steve: Any five-way resonance of unity, order, chaos, idea and stuff is a being?

Amy: Yes.

Steve: What is stuff?
Tim: Anything with mass.
Steve: Five ways. That's remarkable.
Tim: What remark would you make?
Steve: Well, physicists have this thing they call the three body problem. If you have two objects in motion around each other, you can calculate future motion exactly. But if there are three bodies, you can calculate pretty darn closely, but never exactly. With four bodies all bets are off, and five bodies are right out. A five-way resonance is incalculably complex.
Tim: Unity, order, chaos, idea and stuff are not bodies. They do not exist by themselves. Existence requires resonance of all five.
Steve: But the principle of complexity is still relevant. If you modeled the five-way interaction mathematically, it would be way too complex to accurately predict exactly how anything would be in the future. Future possibilities would be practically infinitely complex. There would be no bounds on potential harmonies in a five way resonance.
Tim: We need a graphic.

Tim reached into his sleeve and tossed a tiny glowing firefly-like object off to his side. A large screen appeared in the air and landed gently on eight barely visible spindly seven-jointed legs.

Steve: How did you do that?
Tim: What, you mean the adaptive screen?
Steve: Yes, how did you make that big screen appear from out of your sleeve?
Tim: You've not seen adaptive screens before?
Steve: No!

Tim and Amy appeared shocked. They had the same tense and fearful look as when I asked about the trick campfire and the informed consent form.
Tim: I thought…
Amy, with a hand over her mouth: Woops.
Amanusince: This was really, really weird. Maybe the expanding screen was some new technology, and not an illusion. Maybe these two graduate students hung around their geeky friends so much they didn't even know their cutting edge technology wasn't widely released. At least I had never seen such a screen before. I gave my head an imaginary shampooing. What was the connection with the bioluminescent spider? Was the spider an illusion, too?

Tim and Amy both looked terrified. If their illusions were not part of their research project, that meant they had bumbled their treatment of me. By the looks on their faces and how they shifted nervously in their camp chairs, it was obvious to me they thought they had blown their research project. The illusions must

be essential to their project. I felt sorry for them. After all, this Ambassadors of Thought World routine and the illusions were really interesting and amusing. I wanted to see the wacky experiment through, especially to hear more about this whole infinite one creation myth.
Steve: Look, never mind. The screen is slick. I like it, please continue.

Tim and Amy looked about ready to faint with relief.
Tim: All right, the story was a fable. We pretended the infinite one thinks like a human simply to get ideas across.
Amy: Thought world is part of the infinite one and depends on five-way resonances, too.
Tim: Even though the infinite one might not think at all beyond thoughts of people like you.
Amy: At least not in any way you would recognize as thinking.
Tim: But you think.
Amy: And you are within infinity.
Tim: So the infinite one is a thinking character in our creation myth.
Amy: The creation myth describes why thinking beings have to find harmony in the waves.
Tim: A good example of harmony is when you can find the right words in the right order to express exactly what

you mean.
Amy: Your thought can resonate with the thought of others if you find harmony through language.
Tim: Okay, now on to the diagram. This drawing is also a story, a way of making concepts seem real. Please understand that I am presenting a mental model that has no physical properties.
Steve: Okay.
Tim: Good. Start with the three aspects of infinity: unity, order, and chaos. Now I will draw waves that go through and connect them. Remember, this is nothing physical. Unity, order, and chaos are aspects of infinity. That means that any of them can be in the place of any of the others at any time. They have no body, no time, no scale. They propagate at infinity. They are everywhere at once.
Steve: The mutual attraction and repulsion create the infinite waves.
Amy: Yes. But if you tried to find unity, order, or chaos, there would be nothing there, except in your imagination. They are there, but are not real. Because they propagate at infinity.

Tim's drawing looked like this:

Tim: Resonance of unity and order creates idea. So at the intersection of the waves of unity and order, I will draw a transverse wave to represent idea. Idea waves are resonances of unity and order.

Amy: Idea waves propagate at inflation.

Tim: Inflation is the limit the infinite one chooses for the maximum speed idea can propagate. Idea propagates at inflation, but the effects of idea in the real world propagate at the speed of stuff. The speed of stuff is the speed of light.

Amy: Which means the speed of idea is inflated beyond anything a being like you can perceive.

Tim: Now I'll draw a wave transverse to the intersection of the waves between order and chaos. This represents the resonance that makes stuff. Stuff waves are resonances of order and chaos.

Amy: Stuff propagates at the speed of light.

Tim's drawing now looked like this:

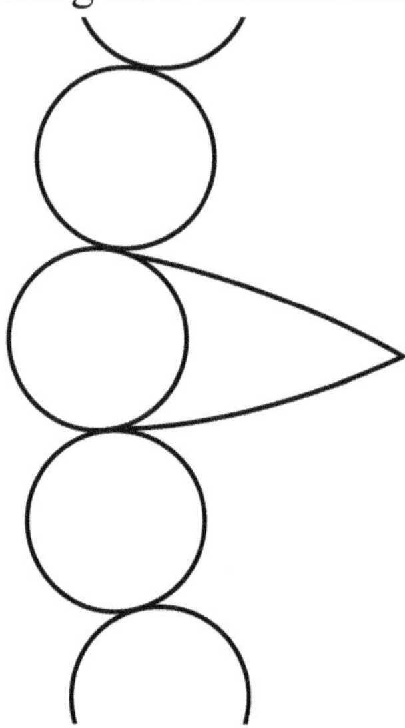

Tim: The idea waves are resonances of order and unity. The stuff waves are resonances of order and chaos. Every resonance of idea and stuff is a being.

Amy: The immediate cause of being is resonances of idea and stuff.

Tim: But the idea and stuff are themselves resonances of unity, order, and chaos. Taken all together, with labels now, Penyu Tortue's story of being looks like this:

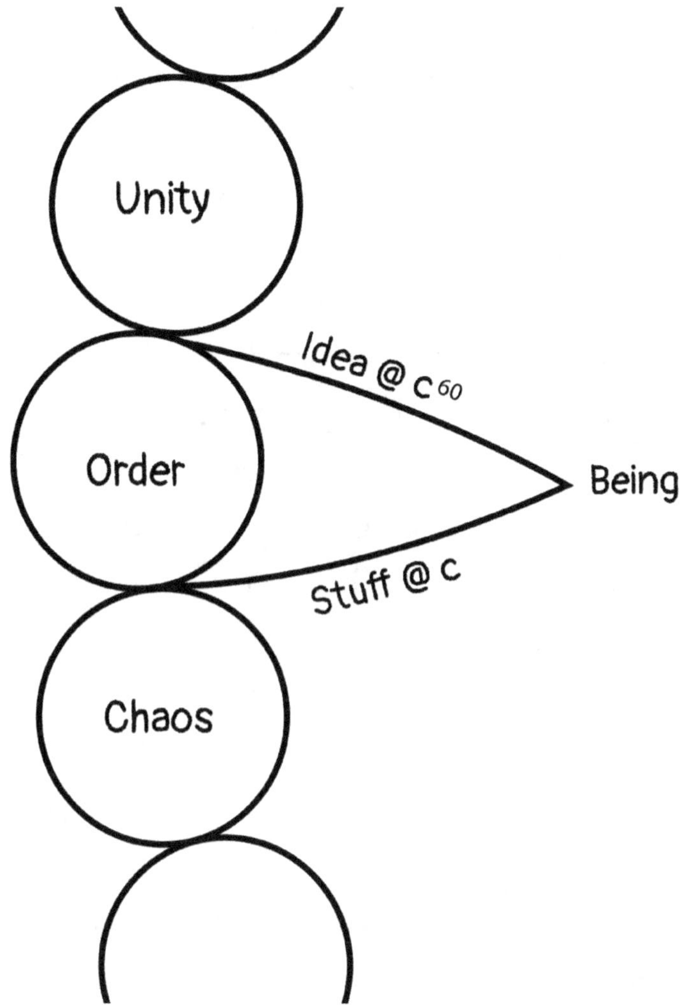

Amy: In the real world, resonances of unity, order, chaos, idea and stuff become beings.

Tim sprang up, threw his arms wide, and robustly burst into song:

The universe is a resonance,
The Milky Way is a resonance,
The sun is a resonance,

Earth is a resonance,
Your environment is a resonance,
You are a resonance
Because your cells resonate
Because your molecules resonate
Beyond which is the irrelevantly small.

Flaps and rustles accompanied the song as frightened animals fled Tim's performance.

Amy: Picture thought world as the cone between order and being, except there is no physical existence in this model, so there is not actually a cone. It is an imaginary cone.

Tim: There are no physical waves beyond being. Yet the theoretical space between being, order, idea and stuff represents thought world.

Amy: Thought world cannot exist without beings.

Steve: You said any time there is a five way resonance, a being exists.

Tim: Yes.

Amy: Among beings that matter at your scale, photons and electrons are the simplest.

Tim: Photons and electrons are simple resonances of unity, order, chaos, idea and stuff.

Amy: That's why photons and electrons are fundamental to all existence.

Tim: There are neutrinos, too, but they don't really count.

Steve: Why not?

Tim: Because neutrinos do not resonate with the real world you exist in.

Amy: Gazillions of them zip right through you all the time, but neutrinos have no effect.

Tim: Practically speaking, at your scale of being, molecules are the smallest beings that you need to concern yourself with. Not that knowledge of subatomic particles is useless. Knowledge about radiation is helpful.

Amy: Other than radiation, though, you can disregard resonances smaller than a molecule.

Tim: Unless you're a physicist or some other geeky meddler in tiny world.

Amy: If you imagine the scales of being musically, they are like octaves.

Steve: Being exists in musical octaves?

Amy: It's an analogy. Molecules are the smallest octave. Subatomic particles resonate at frequencies too small to count. Particles are only relevant if they resonate at the molecule octave. The next octave is cells. Then organisms.

Tim: The organism octave, the one you live in, is within your environment octave.

Amy: Your environment octave is within the Earth octave.

Tim: Earth octave is within the solar system octave.

Amy: The largest octave that you can clearly perceive is galaxies.

Tim: Beyond that is the cosmic pulse.

Steve: Are there octaves beyond the cosmic pulse?

Amy: That is impossible to know.

Tim: If there are, they are beyond your perception.

Amy: All being you can perceive is within our cosmic pulse.

Steve: You are saying that at all octaves, the waves resonate to create beings at the scale of that octave.

Amy: Correct.

Steve: The resonances of unity, order, chaos, idea and stuff are at every scale.

Tim: Yes. The model of being from our creation myth is scale invariant.

Steve: Being always includes chaos?

Tim: Yes.

Amy: No chaos, no being.

Steve: Chaos seems such a negative thing.

Tim: It is part of infinity's nature to disperse, spread, expand, splinter. Variety, diversity, chaos are words that express different perspectives on the expanding aspect of infinity. That is the nature we label chaos. But whether you call it chaos or variety or diversity, chaos is essential to being.

Steve: So you would be okay with calling expansion

variety?

Tim: Sure, when the word variety fits better than the word chaos.

Steve: Variety just sounds better.

Tim: To you.

Steve: Yes.

Tim: Okay. When it fits, we shall call chaos variety.

Steve: So the interaction of unity, order, variety, idea and stuff is the reason there is something rather than nothing. And the reason I am, the reason I exist.

Tim: That is correct.

Steve: I am one resonance of unity, order, variety, idea and stuff within these infinite waves.

Tim: Yes, that is what makes you a being.

Amy: One being within infinity.

Tim: Infinity is perfectly universal, consistent, and open. It has no boundaries, no scale, no limits, no time. It is everywhere at once and purely continuous. It is not a being. It is the source of being.

Amy: Infinity can be difficult to wrap your brain around since everything you can perceive as a living organism has a beginning and an end. The characteristics of infinity are profoundly counterintuitive. Touch the tips of your thumb and fingers in one of your hands.

I did as Amy said, and touched my fingertips with the tip of my thumb.

Amy: What do you get when you touch together the tip of your thumb and fingertips?
Steve: I guess it looks kind of like a cell. An egg could fit in there.
Tim: How much of infinity is within the space where the egg could be?
Steve: Uh, I don't know what to say.
Amy: The answer is all of it. Infinity is pure unity, indivisible. Infinity is outside of time and space, and has no scale. The infinity within that imaginary egg in your hand is truly equivalent to the infinity inside a living Tyrannosaurus Rex or to the infinity in the atmosphere of a planet far, far away.
Tim: So it obviously makes no sense to describe infinity in physical terms.
Amy: Infinity is not a physical thing.
Tim: It is, but it is not a being.
Amy: Infinity is the infinite one.
Steve: I cannot hold infinity in my hand. But an egg is a harmonic resonance of unity, order, variety, idea and stuff in the infinite waves.
Tim: Exactly.
Amy: Beings are resonances of the infinite waves.
Steve: Why aren't people aware of these resonances that cause reality?
Tim: What do you mean? People perceive waves all the

time. It’s fundamental to how you know anything.
Amy: Waves can be potential, or theoretical, and not have any physical existence. But they can still exist in thought world.
Steve: You lost me. What do you mean by a theoretical wave in thought world?
Tim: Okay, let’s describe a concrete example of a theoretical wave in thought world. What’s an animal one would see in these woods?
Steve: There are lots of chipmunks.
Tim: How large is this forest?
Steve: I’m not sure, several square miles.
Tim: Can we just pick one square mile, and imagine we are in the middle?
Steve: Sure.
Tim, gesturing with his hands in the air: All right, picture a graph. We can plot our count of chipmunks on the vertical axis, and time on the horizontal axis. The graph represents the number of chipmunks in our square mile. How many do you think there are right now?
Amanueneses: I felt disappointed that Tim skipped the magic screen and was using a finger in the air. I could follow what he meant okay, but that screen was cool.
Steve: No idea.
Tim: Guess. It doesn’t matter, we just need a scale to work with.

Steve: I don't know, two thousand?

Amy flamboyantly fingered 2000 on the imaginary graph.

Tim: Does the number of chipmunks stay the same throughout the year?

Steve: Unlikely.

Tim: What would cause changes?

Steve: Number of foxes or owls, how many acorns the oak trees drop, unusual weather. Lots of things. How many slugs there are to eat.

Amy: Ew.

Tim: Okay, we will start here at two thousand, say in October. The population will probably go down some over the winter, right?

Steve: Probably.

Tim: Then go up in spring when baby chipper pups are born?

Steve: Sure.

Tim, tracing a wave in the air with his finger: If I plot a graph of chipmunk population over time, the line representing chipmunk population would be like this wave.

Amy: So if you had that wave representing population changes, what would it tell you if in year six the wave went way down?

Tim pointed his finger down to the leaves on the

forest floor.

Steve: Something happened in the chipmunks' environment. Maybe someone cut down a lot of the oak trees, or a fire, or a super bad winter. Or a slug hater wiped out a food source. It could be lots of things.

Amy gave me a look that made me feel uncomfortably like a dry twig.

Tim: But the wave on the graph would give you useful information about the chipmunk population?

Steve: Yes.

Amy: That's what theoretical waves are all about.

Tim: The wave on our graph has no reality aside from what we created. Yet it represents something real.

Amy: Something real that contains information.

Tim: Do the chipmunks care about the graph?

Steve: Of course not.

Tim: If I extended our model wave on the graph into the future, would it have any impact on the chipmunks?

Steve: You mean if you just made something up? Predicted things that you cannot really know will happen?

Tim: Yes.

Steve: That's silly, of course your wave model of the future would not affect the chipmunks. There's a chance the plotted wave would reflect reality, but it would be only coincidence.

Amy: The wave representing chipmunk population is a theoretical wave. Theoretical waves reflect reality, but are not real and cannot affect stuff.

Tim: Unless a being turns the theoretical waves into thoughts and acts on those thoughts in the being's environment.

Amy: Beings like you are able to turn thoughts into reality, you see.

Steve: I am able to turn a thought into reality if my actions resonate in my environment. Like how scientists and engineers use math models to design things.

Tim: Right. If you are in tune with reality, you are able to turn theoretical waves . . .

Amy: Thoughts, that is.

Tim: . . . into real things.

Amy: Theoretical waves exist like the future exists. Tell me, Steve, does the future exist?

Steve: No, not really. I mean the future exists in the sense that we know the future is coming. Sometimes we can predict some of what will be. Like the Earth will keep spinning so the sun always comes up.

Tim: But one can never know for sure exactly what will be in the future.

Steve: Right.

Amy: So the future is there. You'd best pay some attention to it. But right now the future does not exist.

Tim: Theoretical waves are like the future that way. They are there, but do not exist.

Amy: Except in thought world.

Steve: These theoretical waves propagate at inflation?

Tim: Yes, as idea. But idea is resonance of unity and order. Unity and order propagate at infinity. Which means that thoughts are potentially infinite if they resonate with unity and order.

Amy: But thoughts of beings can propagate no faster than the speed of idea.

Steve: I have never heard of such a thing as a speed of idea.

Tim: The limit on the speed of idea is fundamental to being, even though the limit on propagation of idea is not relevant at the scale of organisms like you.

Amy: Not relevant in the same way that the force that holds atomic nuclei together is not relevant at your scale.

Tim: Even though if there were no strong force, you could not exist.

Steve: So at what scale is this limit on the speed of idea relevant?

Tim: Two scales. The smallest and the largest.

Amy: The tiniest particles that can be and the cosmic pulse.

Tim: Resonances of idea and stuff have size limits because idea and stuff have propagation limits.

Steve: How so?

Tim: Harmonic resonances can only occur at certain ratios of propagation.

Amy: Similar to how musical harmonies are ratios of sound frequencies.

Tim: At the very beginning, our cosmic pulse expanded at the speed of idea until a harmonic ratio was reached with the speed of stuff.

Amy: That's why there was a very brief period of inflation at the start of what you call the Big Bang.

Steve: Inflation was the blip before the first harmonic resonance of idea and stuff.

Tim: Yes.

Steve: Okay, let me guess. The lowest limits on how small anything can be are also ratios of idea waves and stuff waves.

Tim: Correct.

Amy: The ratio . . .

Tim: . . . or ratios . . .

Amy: . . . are why particles cannot be infinitely small.

Tim: The ratio or ratios limit how small real things can be.

Steve: What are the ratios?

Tim: We don't know.

Amy: But whatever the ratios may be, from second-hand evidence we think the speed limit of idea is about sixty magnitudes the speed of stuff.

Tim: The speed of stuff is the speed of light.

Amy: Sixty magnitudes faster than light is speed of idea.

Tim: We call the second-hand evidence for the speed of idea the spooky inflation hypothesis.

Steve: Why?

Tim: The only way to detect the limit on idea is from echoes at the boundaries of being.

Amy: Spooky stuff happens when you press right up against the beginning of our cosmic pulse and up against the smallest of the small.

Tim: The quantum world seems so weird because when you press hard enough against particles, you can perceive reflections or echoes of idea waves and stuff waves.

Amy: Even though the idea waves and stuff waves by themselves do not exist.

Tim: Which is why their echoes behave so weirdly relative to the real world you are used to.

Amy: Anyway, when you press hard enough on the boundaries of the cosmic pulse and of quanta, you can find echo evidence of the speed of idea.

Steve: How could you prove this spooky inflation hypothesis?

Tim: Measure entanglement of polarized photons to be at about sixty magnitudes the speed of light. Or whatever the inflation speed of light turns out to be. I suspect that

sixty magnitudes is only approximate.
Steve: Measure entanglement happening at sixtyish magnitudes the speed of light. That would provide evidence that idea propagates at that speed, and not infinity.
Tim: Correct. According to the spooky inflation hypothesis.
Steve: When I think, am I thinking at sixty magnitudes the speed of light?
Tim: No. Your thought propagates at the speed of your nerve impulses. Which is a maximum of about one hundred eighty miles per hour.
Tim: Compared with the speed of idea, nerve impulses are really, really slow.
Amy: Like frozen in time slow.
Steve: Seems fast enough to me.
Tim: That is because the speed of your thought is in order for your scale of being.
Amy: Your speed of thought is in harmony with your organism octave.
Steve: Let me ask you this. Say theoretically people could learn to control idea waves. If people can control waves, people can use the waves to communicate information. If people could control idea waves, would it be possible to communicate at sixty magnitudes the speed of light?

Tim: People cannot control idea waves.

Steve: What about your spooky inflation hypothesis?

Tim: The spooky inflation hypothesis is just a conjecture about the speed of idea. To directly measure inflation you would have to make idea real.

Amy: Which is impossible, because idea cannot exist without resonance with stuff.

Tim: So you would have to measure something that does not exist. Like Amy says, that is impossible.

Anmaneuses: I was starting to wonder whether this anthropology experiment was really some sort of exploratory study. Maybe Tim and Amy were testing out their hypotheses. Floating ideas to find out if their ideas resonate with people like me. I massaged my brow. It occurred to me that one of those hypotheses might be that conscious thought depends on life.

Steve: May I change the subject?

Amy: Sure.

Steve: Can conscious thought exist without life?

Amy: No.

Tim: Conscious thought requires living organisms.

Amy: Living organisms evolve from unbounded harmonies of unity, order, chaos, idea and stuff.

Tim: Heredity expresses unity. Variation expresses chaos. Selection expresses order.

Amy: And heredity, variation, and selection drive the

evolution of self-conscious organisms.

Steve: Fine, but that does not explain how life began on Earth.

Amy: My, would that not be nice to know.

Tim: The beginning of life on Earth is mysterious. It is knowable in principle. But it happened so very long ago. There is not enough direct evidence to know for sure how life started on Earth. But however life started, you can be assured it was due to harmonic resonances of unity, order, variety, idea, and stuff.

Amy: Steve, what do you know about embryology?

Steve: You mean the study of how baby organisms develop?

Amy: Yes.

Steve: Very little. I have read a little about it, and a bit of embryology was included in a biology class I took.

Amy: What do you remember about how a fertilized egg becomes an organism like you?

Steve: My takeaway is how amazing it is that such a complex organism can develop so quickly.

Tim: Kind of mysterious, isn't it?

Steve: Yes. I mean, not so much in the overall concept of how it all works. But if you think about the complexity of what is actually going on, the development of an embryo is pretty awe inspiring.

Amy: But it is all simply coded in the DNA, right?

Steve: Yeah but still, how do all those codes get turned into a real being in such a short time? How do all those chemical signals and everything not get all mixed up? After all, things can and do go wrong. Not every living being develops successfully.

Amy: Well the big picture answer to how life started is harmony of unity, order, variety, idea, and stuff. But you are right. How the details all work is pretty mysterious.

Tim: Not that the details are unknowable. In principle, with omniscient perception one could figure out exactly how a living being develops.

Amy: But in practice, the development of a living organism is so intricate that the details cannot be known in full.

Tim: Yet somehow, like embryos know how to develop, life knows how to start.

Amy: You see, Steve, on planets in friendly stellar environments, life starts and evolves into organisms.

Tim: The organisms evolve toward complexity.

Amy: The more boundless the potential harmonies are in the environment, the more complex the organisms may become. In environments conducive to life, some organisms become so complex they are able to navigate the boundless harmonies by voluntary choice.

Tim: These very special beings are so practically infinitely complex, their harmonies of idea and stuff connect them with thought world.

Amy: The practically infinitely complex beings coexist in real world and thought world.

Tim: These unique harmonic resonances of idea and stuff can think. Because they can think, these beings can perceive and reflect upon their environments. Ability to perceive and reflect on harmonic resonances of idea and stuff enables these creatures to embody thought world. Their ability to navigate complexity by voluntary choice endows them with great creativity.

Amy: These creative organisms have evolved to live in thought world as self-conscious instances of the infinite one.

Steve: What are these special organisms like?

Tim and Amy stared right through me.

Steve: No, please tell me. What are these creative organisms like that can navigate infinite complexity? What do they look like? How do they make choices? Can I meet one of these unique instances of the infinite one?

Tim looked up at the canopy of leaves and sighed. Amy rubbed her temples with her fingers. Tim and Amy looked at each other and shook their heads. Then both of them shook their heads more as they studied the canopy of leaves overhead. Amy looked back at me and shook her head yet again.

Amy, disgusted: I cannot believe it. We get a unique

chance to be ambassadors to a self-conscious instance of the infinite one, and he turns out to have the self-awareness of a turtle.

Steve: What, you mean the special organism that can navigate infinite complexity is *me*?

Amy: Yes, turtle brain, you.

Tim: Do you see any other thinking organisms around you creating and using the internet, for example?

Steve: Well yeah, actually, there was that chimpanzee famous for his photographic self-portraits . . .

Tim interrupted: Never mind. The point is you are for all practical purposes infinitely complex. That's what makes you capable of navigating the boundless harmonies as well as you do. You can think.

Amy: You can imagine!

Tim: You create!

Amy: First you create in your mind. Then if possible, you can make what you imagine real.

Steve: You're calling me a unique instance of the infinite one.

Amy: Yes.

Steve: But I am finite as can be. How can you say that I am practically infinitely complex?

Tim: Are you kidding me? Look at yourself! You are made of about forty trillion cells. And every cell is made of like a hundred trillion atoms. Those trillions of atoms are exquisitely ordered. Your forty trillion cells are organized into an amazingly complex system of organs, systems, and communications. You have a gazillion nerves firing all the time, and thousands of different chemicals relaying a gazillion messages from one part of your body to another.

Steve: How many is a gazillion?

Tim: More than you can count or comprehend.

Amy: The gazillion complexity all works together to keep you alive and let you do all the things you choose to do in your life.

Tim: You are definitely a practically infinitely complex organism.

Amy: Imagine yourself at the octave of the cosmic pulse.

Tim: The scale of the universe.

Amy: You are like forty trillion galaxies of one hundred trillion suns each.

Tim: You do not perceive them because they are so tiny. The cells are like galaxies within you, and the molecules are like suns within your cells.

Amy: But as you said, your pulse of being is one finite organism. You turn your environment of trillions of cells and many trillions of atoms into one you. It's just amazing.

Tim: For the beings that exist within you, you are the creation.

Amy: Even though you're just one tiny finite being in a practically infinitely complex world.

Steve: Infinitely complex world?

Tim: Trust me. If you are not aware that the environment you live in is infinitely complex, you are simply not paying attention.

Steve: So I am an instance of the infinite one, but I am infinitesimally small. Which is it?

Amy: Equally and simultaneously both.

Steve: You are saying I am the infinite one.

Tim: Correct.

Amy: You are also an infinitesimally small speck, a single unit of being in the membrane of life within the field of infinite complexity.

Steve: Both at once.

Tim: It's the paradox of being.

Steve: I am simultaneously the infinite one and an infinitesimally small speck of being. And my organism, my being, can never be more than one unit of being. I am one unique resonance in the infinite waves.

Amy: One amazingly complex resonance of unity, order, variety, idea and stuff.

Tim: One unique, practically infinitely complex organism.

Amy: Your resonance in the infinite waves is the unique you.

Tim: One and only.

Amy: You are a unique resonance.

Tim: Unique means one and only.

Amy: There is only one you. Always. Forever.

Tim: Without exception.

Amy: There will always be only one you.

Steve: I am one unique resonance of being.

Amy: Yes, Steve, why do you keep going on about it?

3.
Belong

Tim: Amazingly complex processes that keep you alive do not require you to think about them.

Amy: Most of what your brain does is unconscious.

Tim: What you think about is a tiny fraction of what your mind does to keep you healthy.

Amy: And much of what keeps you alive happens without input from even the unconscious parts of your mind.

Tim: If you had to consciously think about everything to keep you alive, you would die very quickly.

Amy: That is why you are nowhere anything like all-knowing.

Tim: When it comes to yourself.

Amy: Or anything else.

Tim: You have some control over yourself. But you do not know about or even sense the majority of what is going on to keep you a living human being.

Steve: I don't know about that. I mean, I eat and drink and sleep and keep myself warm. Seems like I have a lot of control.

Tim: Yeah? Well tell me, what does your pancreas do?

Steve: It controls the level of sugar in my blood. I think.

Tim: That is a simplification, but okay. What else does your pancreas do?

Steve: I am not sure.

Amy: You have a vital organ and you do not know what all it does?

Steve: Um, no.

Amy: See our point about your lack of knowledge and control over your being?

Tim: We are not even talking about individual cells.

Amy: Your pancreas is a major organ vital to your life, but you cannot consciously control it.

Tim: If your pancreas is working properly, you cannot even feel it.

Steve: So if I am a unique instance of the infinite one, are you saying that the infinite one is also not aware of most of what goes on within infinity?

Tim: Well, that is impossible to know.

Amy: You and the infinite one exist in different ways.

Steve: The way I think might not be how the infinite one thinks.

Tim: The infinite one might not think at all.

Amy: Infinity's state of being may not be anything like thinking.

Tim: Remember, infinity has no scale. You exist at the

organism scale.

Amy: Infinity has no time. You live in time.

Steve: But if I am a unique instance of the infinite one at my scale in my time, doesn't it make sense that the way I work mirrors the way everything works?

Amy: Perhaps.

Tim: You have billions of brain cells that work together as you. What if one brain cell declared "I am Steve!" What would you say to it?

Steve: Well, actually I have no way to directly communicate with one brain cell. In fact, I cannot even imagine how I would communicate with an individual brain cell.

Tim: We can make that happen.

Aminuciance: This anthropology or psychology experiment Amy and Tim were doing on me was getting more amusing all the time. It was fun to play along. I was curious, what trick would they pull to let me pretend to communicate with one of my brain cells?

Steve: So randomly pick a brain cell and interview it?

Tim: Sure.

Steve, laughing: Okay, let's do it.

Tim: All right, first we have to get a count of cells. Are you okay with us simplifying things a little and just counting cells in your cerebral cortex? It's not your whole brain by any stretch of the imagination. But it will work for our purpose.

Steve: I guess so.

Amy: Tim, isn't a formal random selection overkill? Why don't you just make a haphazard pick? What difference does it make?

Tim: No, Steve said randomly pick a cell, so that is what we will do. If we are going to do this, we should do it right.

Amy, gently shaking her head and rolling her eyes: Suit yourself.

Tim: All right. I have to recruit sensors to do the count. Now Steve, what is going to happen here is sensors are going to count the nerve cells in your cerebral cortex. I promise you that it will not harm you in any way. You may feel some odd sensations. Are you okay with that?

Steve: Odd sensation like a spider web wrapped around my skull? Are you sure there is no way this will hurt me?

Tim: Absolutely sure. We are just getting a count of cerebral cortex cells so we can make a proper random selection.

Steve: Okay, go ahead.

Tim: I want you to put your hands on your knees and hold as still as you can. Whatever you do, do not move your hands from your knees. Hold perfectly still.

Steve: Okay.

Tim: Good, the sensors have arrived. We can begin.

Ready?
Amunusance: I was beginning to feel a little nervous, but I put my hands on my knees and sat still. I figured the lowest risk came from just letting things be. Let events unfold how they will.
Steve: Ready.

There were no noises, and nothing dramatic, but my scalp had a really weird sensation like my hair was crawling.
Steve: I feel like my hair is crawling.
Amy: No wonder.
Tim: Don't worry, just keep still and leave both hands on your knees. This will not take long.

The crawling sensation morphed into a subtle feeling of all my hairs standing on end, like goose bumps over my whole scalp. I imagined I was radiating energy, like a star would, only not as hot.
Tim: Okay, done. Now here is what I want you to do. Stand up.

I stood up.
Tim: Take two steps away from the fire.

I took two steps away from the fire.
Tim: Keep your legs straight and bend down to touch your toes.

I kept my legs straight and bent down to touch my toes. As I did so, a few dozen of the bioluminescent screens with eight legs dropped to the ground and scampered out of my sight into the ferns, forbs, and fallen leaves.

Steve, quickly straightening up: Augh! Can I touch my head now?

Tim: Sure.

I vigorously ran my fingers through my hair and massaged my scalp.

Steve: Did I get them all?

Tim: Oh, yes. Believe me, they were as happy as you to be on their way. The sensors did a good job. We have a count of fifteen billion, four hundred sixty-seven million, two hundred one thousand, one hundred and thirty-seven. Now we can randomly select one.

I sat back down. I looked around to be sure the spiders had all gone away. It seemed they had. They were quiet, anyway.

Tim: Amy, can you do the honors?

Amy had been sitting impatiently with arms crossed observing Tim's performance. She appeared relieved to be in charge of the next step. Amy fiddled the fingers of one hand in the other palm.

Amy: Okay, our random selection from 15,467,201,137 is . . .

Tim made a drum roll on his belly with the flats of his fingers and contorted his mouth into a big oval. Tim's drum roll sounded amazingly like it came from a pair of bongo drums.

Amy gave Tim a bewildered look and rolled her eyes again.

Amy: Twelve million, one hundred twenty-one thousand, nine hundred and fifty-nine.

Tim: Excellent! Let us talk with cell 12121959.

Tim picked something from his sleeve and flung it out beside him. The screen reappeared in the air as before.

Amaslowness: A screen of indefinite size. Where did that technology come from? This was like the world's most elaborate anthropology experiment. Or psychology. No matter. Conducted out in the boondocks, no less. In the middle of the night. I felt lucky to be a participant.

Tim: Okay! There it is, cerebral cortex cell 12121959. We'll use some image enhancement to make cell 12121959 stand out from its environment.

A cell with eight axons and dendrites protruding from it appeared on the screen.

Tim: Hello, cell twelve million, one hundred twenty-one thousand, nine hundred and fifty-nine, can you hear me?

The cerebral cortex nerve cell appeared to make a quick contraction.

Ned: What? Who is there? What is happening?

Tim: Brain cell, we are Tim and Amy, Ambassadors of

Thought World. We are here to ask a few questions and convey some important information. We also have a very special guest here with us to meet you.

Ned: Ambassadors of Thought World? Yeah, right.

Tim: No, really.

Ned: What did you call me?

Tim: Cell twelve million, one hundred twenty-one thousand, nine hundred and fifty-nine.

Ned: My name is Arak Ned Spinner. But please call me Ned.

Tim: Okay, Ned. Will you talk with us?

Ned took a few moments to respond.

Ned, slowly and reluctantly: Okay.

Amy: The first thing, Ned, is we need you to promise to tell us the truth to the best of your ability.

Tim: Because if you tell us things that are not true, you cannot know whether what we tell you in return is true or not.

Ned: Okay, I promise to tell the truth.

Amy: Ned, tell us who you are and what you do.

Ned: I am the center of an information processing web. Waves flow through me. I process the waves.

Tim: How do you process the waves?

Ned: Well, most waves I just send on through. Some of the waves, I give them a boost. Bad ones I shut down so they do not go through.

Amy: How do you know which waves are bad?
Ned: I just naturally sense what is good or bad. I have never thought about it, really. I just do what I naturally do.
Tim: Are there others like you in your information web?
Ned: Oh yes, multitudes.
Tim: How many are multitudes?
Ned: I do not know. Multitudes are more than I can count or comprehend.
Tim: Guess.
Ned: One hundred thirty-seven?
Tim: It is more than that, and here to explain is our special guest Steve. Steve, please introduce yourself.

What on earth? I was not expecting this. They told me there would not be a test.

Steve: Hello, Ned, I am Steve.
Ned: Hello, Steve. Tell me who you are and what you do.
Steve: I am a person who eats and drinks and thinks and walks and talks. And visits trees.
Ned: Are you are connected in my web of information?
Steve: Your web of information is part of my thinking. You see Ned, I am much greater than you. In fact, you exist within me as a part of me.
Ned: You are the source of the waves?
Steve: Yes, and of your food, oxygen, and everything you depend on to exist.

Ned: Oh great and marvelous Steve, you are Nucleus of Being?

Steve: Well yes. In a way. Sort of. I think.

Ned: Oh magnanimous one, provider of all my world, I prostrate myself before you! Well in my case that would be more of a flop, but you get the idea.

Steve: No prostrating flop is necessary.

Ned: How then should I pay homage, my Liege, wondrous Chancellor of Ion Channels, Duke of Depolarization, Lord of Axons and Dendrites?

Steve: Process the waves.

Ned: Great Overlord of Organelles, it is truly marvelous of you to exist for my benefit.

Steve: I exist for you? How do you mean, Ned?

Ned: Oh wondrous Emperor of Endoplasmic Reticulum, I am awed that such a great being as you would devote yourself to providing for and watching over me, Arak Ned Spinner, center of the information waves.

Steve: Actually, Ned, there are many others like you that are also part of me.

Ned: Ah yes, the one hundred thirty seven others that share my duties, and lesser ones too I suppose. Great Governor of Glial Cells, we are all most humble in your presence.

Steve: Actually, Ned, there are quite a few more than one hundred thirty-seven. But we chose to talk with you.

Ned: Glory be to nervous energy! I am the chosen one! So tell me, how many unfortunate unchosen others like me are there?
Steve: Well, just counting my cerebral cortex, fifteen billion, four hundred sixty-seven million, two hundred one thousand, one hundred and thirty-seven.
Ned: Wonder of wonders. I shall pay homage by counting my fellow cerebral cortex cells. One, two, three, four…
Steve: Ned, stop. We don't have time for that.
Tim: It would take about three thousand nine hundred years to complete that task.
Steve: So please stop.
Ned: Of course, Exalted Endoneurium! As you say, Captain of Capacitance! Oh marvelous me! I am the chosen one! Focus of all the great and wonderful Steve's thoughts and energies. Oh happy life of mine! The chosen one!
Steve: Ned, being chosen does not mean that you are the only one. I have many others. You do not have my undivided attention.
Ned: Oh woe! I have displeased the all-powerful Patriarch of Potassium Pumps! I must pay penance. I shall scourge myself!

Ned whipped himself with an axon, enough to cause some cytoplasm to leak out of contusions in his soma.

Steve: Ned! Stop! Do not do that. Whipping yourself is not helpful.
Ned: Catastrophe! The Sovereign Imperator of Neurotransmitters is angry with me! I must make sacrifices!

Ned made a straining sound like he was on the toilet with a bad case of constipation.
Steve: Ned, what are you doing?
Ned, groaning in a way that appeared exceedingly painful: Sacrificing organelles for the greatness of you, my personal Sultan of Sodium, Potentate of Potassium, Czar of Chloride!
Steve: Well stop, okay?
Ned: Yes, as you say, Master of Myelin.

Ned appeared to relax. As he did so, he let out an epic fart. Ned was momentarily obscured by bubbles in his surrounding cerebrospinal fluid.
Aminanuscents: Thank goodness the aroma of his effervescence did not exist at my scale.
Steve: And enough with the flowery language. I don't even know what you're saying half the time. Please call me just Steve.
Ned: Yes, Just Steve! Judge of all I can perceive, Swami of Seratonin, Guardian of Glutamate, Earl of Epinephrine. I shall call you Just Steve forever more. With your permission, Just Steve, may I ask a humble

question of the great Just Steve?
Steve, sighing: Yes, Ned.
Ned: What must I do to ensure everlasting life?
Steve: Well, Ned, you can't. You see, someday I will die. And when that happens, you will die, too.
Ned: Die?
Steve: Yes, no longer think, cease to be.
Ned, frantic: I must sacrifice myself to save Just Steve from death! Apoptose me now!

Ned stretched his axons and dendrites out to his sides and twisted the top part of his cell to one side and then the other. He violently thrashed back and forth, twisting right and left as best he could with his axons and dendrites stretched wide. Ned's twists and stretches looked even more painful than his constipation.
Steve: Ned, stop! Please stop.
Ned: The phage phase doesn't faze me! My martyrdom magnifies the magnificence of my Master of Myelin!
Steve: I am not going to sacrifice you, Ned. I need you. Dialed down a bit, preferably.
Ned: Yes of course Just Steve, Administrator of Acetylcholine, Caliph of Histamine, Duke of Dopamine, Arbiter of Alliteration, Executor of Exclamation Points! What do you want of me?
Steve: Relax. Be you. Just continue processing the waves like you have always done.

Ned: And what else, Just Steve? How shall I properly express my great esteem for the mighty Just Steve, Magistrate of Mitochondria, Leader of Lysosomes, Great Giver of Glucose?

Steve: No special effort is needed, Arak Ned Spinner. Feel grateful if you will. All I want is for you to do a good job processing the waves. Go on doing the same as what you have always done.

Ned: Yes, Just Steve, but I must express my gratitude for your magnanimous mastery of our domain. Oh great provider of all my needs, I am honored and overwhelmed at being the chosen one. I am forever grateful. As the chosen one I shall make a regular schedule to channel ions in your honor.

Steve, grateful to not have to smell that: If you insist, Ned. I need to go now.

Ned: Yes of course Just Steve, Nucleus of Being. Just Steve must be very busy attending to your multitude of cells, even greater than one hundred thirty-seven. Your multitudes are more than I can count or comprehend.

Steve: Yes thank you Ned. I wish you nervous electrical imbalances for as long as you shall be.

Ned: Oh, kinder words have never been spoken, great and honorable Just Steve! I exalt in being the chosen one! How fortunate I am to be chosen by the all-knowing Just Steve, King of Capacitance, Master of Myelin, Deliverer of Dendrites, Great Giver of Glucose . . .

I motioned with my hand back and forth across my throat to signal to Tim to please cut off the connection. The screen went dark. I sat back in my chair, leaned way back, looked overhead, and let out a big sigh.

Steve: That guy was a *lunatic*.

Amy: Oh I don't know. Everything he said made perfect sense from his perspective.

Tim: Yeah. There he is, a cell in a very sheltered environment, and a voice comes out of nowhere shouting "Ambassadors of Thought World here to greet you!"

Amy: How would you react?

Steve: I could try to ignore it.

Amy: You would not be able to.

Tim: Lucky for you, Ned was on your side.

Steve: He didn't know what he was believing in.

Amy: It doesn't matter.

Tim: Ned chose to believe.

Steve: But that's not really me.

Amy: It's your brain. Ned lives inside your brain. It makes perfect sense from Ned's perspective to believe in you the way he did.

Tim: Would you rather Ned think of you as Unjust Steve?

Steve: Well, no, that's not the point.

Amy: Then why fault Ned?

Steve: Okay, so is Ned is part of me, but in no way all of

me. But he does not know that.

Tim: Could you survive without that cell?

Steve: Yes, I guess any one cell is not significant to my life. It's only when a whole bunch of cells get sick or die that it affects me.

Tim: Right. Now tell me, what chance does Ned have of knowing what you are thinking right now?

Steve: None, really. The firing of one nerve cell is just a tiny part of my thinking.

Amy: What if Ned argued back, "I cause thinking by letting ions across my membrane when I want them to. The whole mind must be dependent on my work!"

Steve: I would have to tell Ned that no, what you comprehend is just a tiny part of something you have no way of understanding.

Tim: In the same way, you have no more chance of knowing the infinite one's state of being than Ned has of knowing what you are thinking.

Amy: From your perspective it is impossible to know what, how, or even whether the infinite one thinks.

Tim: Nevertheless, you are a unique resonance of the infinite waves.

Amy: Which makes you part of the infinite one.

Tim: Which means your consciousness is of the infinite one.

Frogs croaked. Crickets chirped. An owl hooted.

Stars winked among the canopy overhead.

Steve: So to be, I have to be a harmonic resonance of unity, order, variety, idea, and stuff?

Amy: That's right.

Tim: Your organism and the energy your pulse of being processes are required to maintain harmonic resonance in the infinite waves.

Steve: I end if any of the five resonances are broken.

Tim: Yes.

Amy: No living organism, no unique instance of the infinite one, can exist without harmonic resonance of unity, order, variety, idea and stuff.

Steve: So then death is the end of the pulse of being that is me. The breaking of the resonances that make me a unique being.

Amy: Yes, resonances like any pulse of being.

Tim stood up and enthusiastically broke into song:

The universe is a pulse of being
The Milky Way is a pulse of being
The sun is a pulse of being
Earth is a pulse of being
Your environment is a pulse of being
You are a pulse of being
Because your cells are pulses of being
Because your molecules are pulses of being
Beyond which is the irrelevantly small.

Tim danced around his chair as he sang. Amy looked on approvingly. The few remaining frightened animals made rustling noises as they fled Tim's performance.

Steve: If I am made of molecules, am I then the same as every other being? Aren't molecules all exactly the same? I mean, a water molecule is a water molecule, right? I duplicate what surrounds me. In your words, a pulse of being is a pulse of being.

Amy: You are made of a gazillion molecules, so your pulse of being is unique.

Tim: Besides, even if molecules of a type may be the same, each individual molecule is a unique resonance of idea and stuff.

Amy: Every molecule occupies its own time and space as a unique resonance of being.

Tim: Every being is a unique resonance in the infinite waves, whether the being is a molecule, cell, organism, environment, star, or galaxy.

Steve, looking up at stars peeking among the leaves: It's all infinite waves. And I am a unique resonance of those waves.

We sat quietly for a while. Those stars among the leaves captivated me. The night was warm and pleasant. Not muggy, slight breeze. Moonlight competed with the stars among the countless leaves. A short distance east fireflies swarmed in a clearing formed by the fallen body of a great tree. Each fly glowed for a moment, then faded, then glowed again. The fireflies were moving in glows that formed gently seething pulses of orange light.

Amy: If it were possible to view thinking organisms in thought world from the outside, I think it might look something like that swarm of pulsing orange fireflies.

Steve: Don't pulses of being begin much more dramatically than the glowing of those fireflies?

Tim: Maybe. If I'm following Amy's reasoning, what the fireflies best represent is the glow of thought that emanates from life in galaxies within cosmic pulses. Did I get that right, Amy?

Amy: Tim's got my drift. The fireflies are like glowing instances of life. Galaxies host life. Life creates self-conscious beings.

Steve: Are you saying thought is a type of bioluminescence?

Amy: It's an analogy.

Tim: Like the glow of the fireflies, life in galaxies takes some time to get started, glows for a while, then fades.

Amy: Galaxies, stars, planets and environments come and go. But it makes sense that somewhere within infinity there are always glows of life, thought, and consciousness.

Steve: Individual flies turn on and off, but the swarm as a

whole keeps glowing.

Amy: Right. The fireflies reflect the swarm of thinking organisms in our cosmic pulse of being.

Tim: My guess is that if infinity thinks, it is the glow of thoughts generated by individual living organisms.

Amy: Individual fireflies that come and go.

Steve: Hey look! Over there below the fireflies is a frog on the ground under the swarm. There's a shaft of moonlight lighting him up like an actor on stage.

On cue, the frog shot his tongue up and nabbed a firefly.

Tim: Bang! Got one.

Amy: Does the swarm look any different?

Steve: No. One down is not enough to tell any difference.

The frog didn't move. I imagined the frog was chewing, until I realized that frogs do not chew. Crickets chirped. An owl hooted. A frog's croak sounded like a burp.

Tim: Well, that pretty well covers Penyu Tortues's story about being. Shall we move on to knowledge?

Steve: No, not yet. I want to know more about this cosmic pulse we live in. How did it come to be, and what is beyond it?

Amy: Our creation myth describes how the cosmic pulse came to be. As far as what might be beyond it, that is unknowable.

Tim: This might be the only cosmic pulse of being. What might be beyond is impossible to know.
Steve: But you must have ideas about how many cosmic pulses there might be.
Tim: Can we just move on to knowledge, and not be stuck in conjecture?
Steve: No! You want me to pay attention to your treatment of me as Ambassadors of Thought World. I want to hear your thoughts about where the cosmic pulse fits into everything. I insist. If you do not tell me more, I am going back to my tent.

I petulantly crossed my arms and put on a scowl.
Amanuscious: I sure hoped my act would work. I really wanted to see how they might illustrate what this cosmic pulse was relative to my world. I theatrically sat there looking as serious as I could muster while struggling to not burst out in laughter.

Tim and Amy replied to my arm cross with crosses of their own. Amy looked angry. Tim looked exasperated. We were having a scowling arms crossed standoff.
Tim: I guess we could show him Dr. Penyu's projection.
Amy: We could. I always enjoy visiting Dr. Penyu.
Tim: Steve, do you get motion sickness?
Steve: I'm not prone. If you subject me to extremes, maybe.

4.
Wave

Tim and Amy got up and carried their chairs to an area to my right.

Tim: Steve, come move your chair over here between us.

I did as Tim suggested. I moved to the spot facing away from the campfire into the woods, and set my chair between theirs. We all sat down.

Amy: Okay, we are going on a trip into thought world.

Tim: Try to relax, stay awake, and pay attention.

Steve: Should I click my heels or clap my hands?

Amy and Tim gave me blank stares.

Amy: Uh, no. Do you feel an urge to click your heels or clap your hands?

Steve: Not really. Never mind.

Tim and Amy gave one another quizzical looks. Tim pushed his glasses up and scrunched his nose. Amy cracked her knuckles. Tim made a face like "any idea?" Amy silently mouthed "no clue." Both shook their heads and shrugged their shoulders.

Tim: Now listen, as we transition into thought world you will see things that do not match what your body expects.

Amy: What your inner ears tell you and what your eyes tell you will not match.
Tim: The mismatch can make you feel really, really sick.
Amy: We don't mean a little queasy. We mean dizzy for hours or even sick for days.
Tim: So we need you to wear this.

Tim handed me a hood. It was shaped to cover my eyes, ears and skull, but it left the rest of my face exposed.

Steve: This is really heavy.
Tim: It has webs of lead in it, among other things. That's partly why it's a hood and not just a blindfold. The part over your skull keeps the information barrier from slipping off.
Amy: The hood very effectively shuts out external stimuli, including sound. Sound mismatches can cause you to be sick, too.
Tim: The hood should keep you from getting sick.
Amy: The sudden complete loss of images and sound may make you feel alarmed or anxious. Just relax. You will not have the hood on for long.
Tim: The hood is just for the transition. When we get all the way into thought world you will feel two taps on the tip of an index finger. That's your signal to take the hood off.
Amanuscents: I figured the hood must have been part

of their treatment of me to gather data for their research project. Their study must have included how people respond to having a scary hood on and pretending to be in thought world. Pretty clever, really. A hood that cuts out external stimuli must have psychological effects on anyone. Yet it should be completely harmless. I hoped.

Steve: What are the risks here?

Amy: Well, if you keep the hood on until you feel the two taps, the risk of feeling sick is minimal.

Steve: What other risks are there?

There was a long pause. Amy and Tim gave each other inquiring looks.

Steve: Don't forget our truth pact.

Tim: Well, . . . sometimes . . .

A pause.

Steve: Go ahead, tell me.

Tim, nervously: Some people who go off into thought world do not come back.

Amy, quickly: But that is totally your choice. We won't do anything that would cause that to happen.

Tim: Right. If you were to choose to stay in thought world and not reconnect with real world, it would be one hundred percent your choice.

Steve: But it's possible?

Amy: Yes, it's possible.

Tim: But we absolutely do not want that to happen.

Amy: We will not do anything to prevent you from reconnecting with real world.
Tim: It is vital to us that you do not leave real world behind, actually.
Amy: So you have nothing to fear.
Steve: Okay, let's do it.
Tim: All right, into thought world we go.

The hood was fairly heavy, but surprisingly comfortable. The lead webbed hood did an impressive job of eliminating sight and sound. It was like one of those cave tours where they turn off the lights, only without noises from others on the tour.

We accelerated. Our sense of speeding forward was gradual at first. The pressing against our backs became steadily greater. It was like taking off in an airplane, except the sense of acceleration was stronger and lasted longer. For a few moments we shuddered like we were driving on a washboarded gravel road. Small bumps at first. Then more jarring. Just when the vibration began to feel uncomfortable, everything felt smooth again.

Two taps on the tip of my index finger.

I took the hood off. All was black and silent, as if the hood still blocked external stimuli. It was like still being inside a deep cave. Totally dark. Eerily silent. They said to not freak out. Do not freak out.

Tim: Okay, Steve, ready for a ride through thought world? We're going to surf the infinite waves.
Steve, with a tremble in my voice: Is it going to be pitch black the whole time?
Tim: No. Watch.

A dimly lit screen emerged from under the cowl of the compartment we were sitting in and propped itself up on eight legs in front of Tim. Tim tapped the screen twice, then moved his fingers rapidly across the surface. Waves danced around his fingertips. Tim's fingers swirled, pinched, and swept around too fast for me to follow what he was doing. Then the screen scampered back below the cowling.

Red light made it so one could just barely see. Gradually the red light grew orange like early dawn. Around us were countless pale red and orange waves. The loud waves were orange. The quiet waves were red. In my peripheral vision, the pale waves appeared simple and smooth. When I focused my attention on any group of waves, the waves became multicolored and more complex and music began. The music started as a low hum with texture I could not quite put into a tune. I noticed we were no longer in our camp chairs.
Steve: What is this we're sitting in?
Amy: The Wave Rider.

I leaned forward to take a look. Across the front

was painted Wave Rider in bright red letters on an indigo metal flake background. Silvery stars spraying from the letters illuminated the ultramarine field.

Steve: A roller coaster car?

Tim: It's been modified.

Amy: It works.

Aminuscience: I was so impressed by how elaborate this whole experiment was. Amy and Tim must have gotten one heck of a generous grant to put all this together for a graduate research project. A sweet roller coaster car!

At the very moment I was thinking about their psychology study, the waves seemed to become more organized. The waves became smoother, but with higher peaks and troughs. The visions and music had a pulsating, ethereal beauty.

Steve: Tim, what were you doing on the screen there?

Tim: Programming our resonances through the waves.

Amy: Are you ready for a fun ride through thought world?

Steve: You mean am I awake and paying attention?

Tim: And interested?

Iamanuisance: I felt an urge to click my heels and clap my hands, but I restrained myself.

Steve, laughing: Yes.

Tim: Then let's go.

Our Wave Rider roller coaster car crested a smooth

wave and began to move faster. The acceleration was subtle at first. We rode the crest of our sine wave up until we peaked and began to decline. It was like being hurtled forward through time. Except it was all visual, like out of body.

Steve: Hey, are there no seat belts or safety bars?

Amy: Don't worry. Once we get going, you'll be stuck to your seat like negative sticks to positive.

We surfed ahead on a point just ahead of the crest of our sine wave. In one sense we seemed to be going down. But at the same time, the wave grew in height. The result was a sensation of propelling forward. In the pale light the waves surrounding us looked like crystal clear ocean water. Phosphorescent plankton floated around us. The plankton alternated from red to yellow and blue to green.

Tim: It will take us a few moments to get to Dr. Penyu's lagoon. Enjoy the ride. If anything gets to be too much, just speak up. I can calm things down if thrilling trends into frightening. Or sickening.

The remaining red and orange waves beneath us became blue. The tune gained complexity. Wave crests appeared white as the ambient light broke from dawn to daylight. The light came from every direction.

Tim: I'm going to start us out by boosting this nice smooth sine wave. Big amplitude and high frequency at first, then riding out with smaller amplitude and lower frequency. All at up and down orientation from your perspective.

Steve, nervously: Okay.

We rode up, up, up on our spot just in front of the wave peak to far above the surrounding sea of waves. The bioluminescent waves below us glowed in a fractal pattern I had never seen before. The blue, green, red, and yellow pattern became the tune. I could see the music and hear the waves. The sensations were unlike anything I had perceived before.

Next we experienced that special moment on a real roller coaster when you are in the front car looking down a scary steep slope. How many cars are in this train? The clatter of the lifting chain clicks and clicks. One hangs above the downslope, more anxious with each click. Then the clatter stops and the back car releases from the chain.

Amy: Here we go!

We tore down the slope of the wave at a breathtaking pace. I felt the press of gravity at the bottom of the wave, and we lifted up the next slope. Weightless at the top, we careened down a slightly less steep slope and up a longer wave. This repeated, each time gentler and longer. Less steep, longer. It became meditative and relaxing to ride the ever gentler waves. Our pace became a relaxing rock on a gentle swell.

Tim: Okay, now the same thing, only with left and right orientation.

We veered off to one side and climbed a sideways wave. It was a sensation much like before. The acceleration was thrilling. Only instead of cresting a wave and going down, we made a curve zipping off to the side. We felt weightless at the crest of each sideways wave, followed by lateral acceleration. Just like up and down, only side to side. When we reached troughs, I heard swooshing sounds.

Tim: You've got to see this.

Wave Rider rotated so we were looking back from where we came. A great spray rose up from where our roller coaster car carved waves. The spray reflected rainbow colors. We continued the side to side ride on a smooth sine wave of decreasing amplitude and longer frequency. The spray did not come back down like water normally would. Instead, the spray weightlessly spewed endlessly upward. The result was an enormous, brilliantly colored S curve. Shiny waves of multicolored spray filled my field of view. Our pace slowed, but the undulating rainbow kept expanding.

Steve: What kind of waves can you ride in thought world?

Tim: It is all infinite waves.

Amy: Everything that is can be modeled as a wave. It is all infinite waves.
Tim: When you figure out where you are in the infinite waves, you learn who and what you are.
Steve: Can you take us over Niagara Falls without killing us?
Tim: Go over the falls in Wave Rider and not die?
Steve: Ideally.
Tim, laughing: Sure, let's do it!

The screen reappeared and Tim repeated his little finger dance. Suddenly we were floating rapidly along on a broad river of chilly clear water. The rocks and boulders on the riverbed rushed beneath us. A fish swam in a panic upstream. The falls roared. The roar rushed upon us. I felt glad the screen had clambered back to a safe spot. In no time, we were hurtling down through space filled with water and spray.

Amy: Yeeee-hah!

Instead of crashing at the bottom, we curled at the last moment up and out in a sweeping spiral. If this were a movie, Wave Rider would be a helicopter on a daring tour of the falls.

Steve: That was awesome!
Tim: Just a warmup for the DNA Twister.
Amy: Take it easy, Tim. This one makes me dizzy if we go too fast.

Our path appeared to become a rail. We corkscrewed forward. We were surrounded by an alternating pattern of blue, green, red and yellow. The blue was always across green. The red was always across yellow. Patterns seemed to emerge. The patterns seemed familiar somehow. But perceived patterns faded before my attention could make sense of them. We rode the corkscrew for a few dozen loops.

Amy: Tim, can we straighten out?

Tim: Sure.

The screen emerged on cue and Tim did his finger dance. We stopped corkscrewing.

Tim: Are you okay, Amy?

Amy: Yes, but I was beginning to feel a touch dizzy. How are you, Steve?

Steve: I'm all right.

Tim: We'll just quietly sail along for a while, then. No need to make anyone feel sick.

Wave Rider rode gently on the waves. It was like being in a chunky sailboat riding a light breeze.

Steve: This is very pleasant. The wave ride has been exciting, but this is so relaxing. Thank you for minimizing the waves.

Tim: Actually, I smoothed the waves by adding and averaging.

Steve: More waves makes for a smoother ride?

Tim: If you average them out.
Steve: What if you did not average them?
Tim: The dissonance would tear you to itty bitty bits.

As we sailed along the gentle waves, I kept thinking that I saw things. I would see something out of the corner of my eye. But when I turned toward what I saw, it would disappear. In two particular instances I must have jerked my head pretty obviously.

Amy: What is the matter, Steve?
Steve: Are there creatures surrounding us?
Tim: Those are the forms.
Steve: Forms?
Tim: Your mind is forming meaning from resonances it has never perceived before.
Steve: Are they real?
Amy: No. Your mind is trying to make sense of random harmonies in thought world. The theoretical waves are not real. But since you are in thought world, your conscious mind is trying to connect the random harmony with what you normally perceive to be real.
Tim: Thought world is a sea of infinite waves. In a sea of infinite waves, there will always be random harmonies.
Amy: You are perceiving harmonic resonances you have never experienced before. Your mind tries to make sense of the unfamiliar.
Tim: Any time your mind perceives resonances that do

not fit with previous experience, you either imagine something to make the sensation match experience, or you discard the perception.

Amy: You select what to do about sensations and perceptions.

Steve: I see.

Amy: So Steve, what did you see?

Steve: A flying whale and a chicken reading a book.

Tim: A chicken reading a book? Seriously? I mean, a flying whale is like mermaids or dragons or sea monsters. Nothing unusual there. But a chicken reading a book? For real?

Amy: What was the chicken reading?

Steve: *Flags Up!* by Lillian Mountweazel.

Tim: A chicken reading a book. That's the weirdest thing ever.

Steve: Sorry, that's what I saw.

Amy: Let it be, Tim. A chicken read a book. A whale flew over Wave Rider. All is well. We're getting close to Dr. Penyu's lagoon.

Tim: I am going to ride this sweet wave straight through the gap in the reef.

Amy: Are you crazy? You are going to kill us all.

Tim: I've got it.

Amy did not act afraid, despite what she said about getting killed. We surfed along the length of a huge wave.

It was a size of swell that needed much space and time to come to be. The wave continued to grow as we rode along. We picked up speed, racing along the face of the wave as it grew higher and the slope grew steeper. The screen cowered down but stayed in place, gripping fast for dear life. The eight legged screen swiveled about as if intent to watch what happened next.

Steve: What is happening?

Tim: A tube ride on this epic wave, then a hard cut into the tiny opening at just the right moment.

Amy, calmly: He is going to kill us all.

The crest of the massive wave curled up and over us. We became engulfed in the tubular wave. The tube was awesomely large. It seemed on scale with all existence. At least existence I am capable of perceiving. Enveloped in the wave, the only way out I could perceive looked to be dead ahead.

Tim: Here we go!

Wave Rider took a hard right up slope, completed a two hundred and seventy degree turn, and hurtled straight into a tiny split in the water crashing from above. We were engulfed in the roar of our huge wave as we hit a small slit in the reef and squirted into a lagoon. The crashing sound receded behind us.

Amy: Well played, Tim.

Tim, proudly: Thanks. Glad I didn't kill us this time.

We flowed into calm water inside an atoll. It was beautiful. Crystal clear water was home to riotous coral reefs. We were surrounded by low islands bordered in bright white sand. Lush vegetation grew on the land above high tide. The water below us was filled with brilliantly colored organisms of more varieties than I could begin to count.

Tim: Here, let me give you a better view of the marvelous life below us. See that giant green turtle over there? I'll eavesdrop on its visual signals so you can see what the turtle sees.

The spider screen happily rose up, grew larger, and showed us a panoramic view of the life below us. The screen proudly glowed with images of countless colorful creatures. I had seen images of reefs before, but never anything as lush and beautiful as this. The lush life was more than I could comprehend in any one moment. The variety of living beings overwhelmed my senses. The lagoon appeared to be a paradise for the countless beings living there.

Steve: The colors seem different from what I'm used to.

Amy: The turtle's perception of light is shifted to ultraviolet compared to your vision. Tim, go ahead and transpose the images toward red.

Tim made a finger flourish across the screen and some of the fish and corals appeared bright red.

Steve: Ah, that did it. Before I did not see any reds, because I was not able to perceive unfamiliar waves.

We slowly drifted across the lagoon toward a floating dock. Beyond the landing I could see an octagonal, seven story pagoda among misty trees. The pagoda was pretty in an ethereal way. I remained captivated by the life beneath Wave Rider.

Steve: Can you have the turtle swim over to where those birds are circling?

Tim: No can do.

Amy: That is definitely not allowed.

Tim: We can pick up the signals of the turtle's optical nerve impulses. But we have no way to influence the turtle's behavior.

Amy: That would violate the turtle's ability to make its own choices. So we would never try to influence that turtle's behavior, even if it were possible.

Tim: Which it's not. Old turtle has free will.

We continued drifting slowly toward the dock. I was mesmerized by the riot of life below us. Old turtle observed all. There were hundreds of types of coral in all shapes and colors. Thousands of bright invertebrates lived in every nook and cranny. Countless brightly colored fish swam about.

I could not help but wonder what the old turtle thought about paradise. I lost sense of time, and was startled when we bumped into the dock.

5.
Wonder

Amy: Now listen, Steve. This is a rare privilege to visit Dr. Penyu. Pay very careful attention.
Tim: Dr. Penyu is kind and understanding, but has no tolerance for inattention.
Steve: Can I ask questions?
Amy: Yes, but choose your questions carefully. Our time here is limited.
Tim: The good professor's time is very valuable and we are not here to waste a moment of it. Oh, and this is very important. When Dr. Penyu indicates it is time for us to go, we go. Got it?
Steve: Got it.
Amy: One more thing. Dr. Penyu can seem very . . . how should I say this . . . well, . . .
Tim: Let's leave it at that, Amy. There is no need to bias Steve's perception of Dr. Penyu.
Amy: So right.
Tim: But don't let Dr. Penyu's appearance fool you. The good professor's theories are brilliant.

Amy stepped out of Wave Rider and walked down

the floating dock. I followed. Tim was close behind. The octagonal pagoda was nestled among majestic trees. The trees were so dense and moist a misty microclimate shrouded the seven story pagoda in a vaporous cloud. Our path through the lush vegetation momentarily put the building out of sight. The profusion of plants and birds were as diverse and beautiful as the sea life in the lagoon. Butterflies and dragonflies busily fluttered and hummed about us. Brilliantly colored snakes and lizards moved from the path to make room for our steps. I saw a bright green slug and a snail with a bold blue shell. There were countless varieties of spider webs throughout the vegetation. I sensed there were many more webs beyond those I could see. It was a fascinating walk. The serene pagoda came back into view. A framework of eight legs with seven segments each supported delicate membranes. The walls of the pagoda were made of a translucent film filled with math formulas. I did not recognize any of the formulas, but then I am no mathematician. We stepped inside. I imagined I was inside a giant spider. A spider really good at math.

Amy: Dr. Penyu?

A tall, slim woman in a plain white tunic danced on bare feet into the room with arms outstretched. Dr. Penyu wore a gossamer cape that floated far out behind her. The cape was thick as a hand, but almost transparent.

It appeared nearly weightless. Weightless like a spider web. Dr. Penyu danced a hopping, toe-to-heel shuffle in a wide circle around us. Her arms spread out like wings. She seemed pleased to show off the gentle waves of spider web cape flowing behind her as she circled us. Her shuffles and hops caused the cape to dance to her tune. Dr. Penyu's dance brought the spider pagoda to life.

Dr. Penyu: Ah, Tim and Amy. How nice of you to visit. And you have brought a friend.

Tim: Very nice to see you, Dr. Penyu. This is Steve, our guest from real world.

Amy: He is interested in seeing your cosmic projection.

Dr. Penyu continued to dance a hopping trot in a circle around us, her cape floating in tune. The dancing professor gave no indication whether a guest from real world was welcome. I felt a need to say something.

Steve: I love your beautiful cape, Dr. Penyu. I have never seen anything like it.

Dr. Penyu, shuffle hopping along: The spiders made it for me, dear souls. I absolutely adore the way this cape responds to my every move. My spider web cape is beautiful, is it not?

Dr. Penyu continued circling us, showing off the gently undulating layers of spider web echoing her syncopated hops and shuffles. The cape responded like a good musician would.

Steve: Indeed it is, Dr. Penyu.

Dr. Penyu bowed to acknowledge my compliment. As Dr. Penyu straightened up, one corner of the cape drifted up into her face.

Dr. Penyu: Yuck!

Dr. Penyu swiped with one hand to try to get the corner of spider web cape out of her face, which caused the web nearest her hand to whip around into her face, too.

Dr. Penyu: Blech!

Two big swaths of web were now plastered to her face. Dr. Penyu lurched awkwardly forward and to one side. The cape floated up perpendicular to the floor.

Dr. Penyu: Augh!

Inexplicably, Dr. Penyu twirled on the ball of one foot and spun in a jerk. Her spin caused the floating cape of spider web to whip tightly around her body.

Dr. Penyu stood immobile. The cape was wrapped tight. She was trapped in a fresh cocoon of spider web. Dr. Penyu violently wriggled her toes. She otherwise stood motionless. She had no choice but to stand motionless.

Aminauseous: Being cocooned in a web like that must have felt awful. I felt icky just looking at her wrapped up like that.

From inside the cocoon came painful straining

noises. There were bulges from where her elbows would be. Toes wriggled fiercely. Louder straining noises. Slighter bulges. The cocoon appeared to relax. Muted flatulence. The cocoon stood quietly for a moment.

Dr. Penyu, calmly but muffled: How embarrassing. And stinky. Tim, Amy, would you be so kind as to unwrap me?

Tim and Amy at once: Yes, yes, Dr. Penyu, of course!

Amy and Tim sprang forward to help Dr. Penyu out of her cocoon. Amy and Tim had some trouble finding the edges, but with effort they located places to grab hold. Each tugged at the cape. As they peeled the spider web away from the cocooned body of Dr. Penyu, the cape gave a soft noise like tape being pulled from felt. Dr. Penyu stood still and silent as she was being unwrapped. Tim and Amy were able to quickly unwrap the cape once they had found the edges. They stepped away, holding the train of spider web out behind Dr. Penyu's shoulders.

Dr. Penyu: Thank you ever so much. Now I am going to kneel down, and I want you to carefully, gently lift the cape off from over my head.

Dr. Penyu knelt down and put her hands on her knees. Dr. Penyu had attractive hands. Tim and Amy delicately lifted the cape away from Dr. Penyu. Once the cape was free, Dr. Penyu stood up, reached behind her head, and used her beautiful hands to release a luxurious cascade of pure white hair.

Dr. Penyu: Excellent. Now do me a big favor, and run and hang that thing in the big tree with the low branches over where the monkeys live. The one way out of my sight.

Amy: Gladly, Dr. Penyu.

Tim and Amy ran off, the cape flapping vigorously behind them.

Dr. Penyu, combing her beautiful white hair with her fingers: So Steve, do I look more dignified now that I am not encased in a spider web cape?

Steve: You actually made a very elegant looking cocoon, Dr. Penyu.

The professor peered at me with a scowl.

Dr. Penyu: Are you serious or are you mocking me?

Steve: I am serious. Your cocoon was quite beautiful. As are you.

Dr. Penyu: I was not in the mood to chrysalis into a butterfly.

Steve: What mood would that be?

Dr. Penyu: Emergent. I am far too old for that.

I found myself staring at Dr. Penyu's eyes, which were unnaturally blue and shone like silver.

Steve: Dr. Penyu, you have the most remarkable eyes.

Dr. Penyu: What remark would you make about them?

Steve: They remind me of silvery blue glass ornaments.
Dr. Penyu: Yes, that is because I had them silvered.
Steve: Silvered?
Dr. Penyu: I used to have terrible chronic eye infections. So I got my eyes infused with atoms of silver. That's what makes my eyes shine this way. A side effect of the silver is the intense blue of my irises. I always had blue eyes, but not like this.
Steve: Doesn't the silver obstruct your vision? Reflect away the light?
Dr. Penyu: No worse than mild cataracts. Beats the heck out of chronic infections. So you are here to view my cosmic projection. How much did Amy and Tim tell you about it?
Steve: Nothing, really. I insisted I wanted to know more about cosmic pulses. So they offered to bring me to see you.
Dr. Penyu, walking slowly to a very large screen: Why were you so insistent about cosmic pulses?
Steve: Ever since I was a little kid, the thought of infinity has kind of grabbed part of my brain and won't let go. So I am really curious about what infinity is like.

Dr. Penyu froze, turned very slowly and gazed at me with those remarkable silvery indigo eyes.
Dr. Penyu: You mean, you cannot help but think about infinity.

Steve: Not like all the time, or I couldn't function. But off and on, yes. It's like always there. When I think about infinity seems pretty random, to tell the truth.

Dr. Penyu peered intently at me and came toward me until inches from my face. We were eyeball to eyeball.

Dr. Penyu: I am that way too, Steve. I have a theory why.

The professor's eyes were mesmerizing. Up this close, I could not help but notice that her irises were not only ultramarine blue but also spiral. The silver points of light made Dr. Penyu's irises look like sparkly blue spiral galaxies.

Dr. Penyu: You see, Steve, and I must say I am so happy to share this with someone who might believe and understand. This infatuation with infinity that you and I share, you know what that is?

Steve: No, Dr. Penyu.

Amianewsense: Were the silver spirals rotating, or was that an illusion? Her pair of sparkly blue spiral galaxies captivated me as much as what Dr. Penyu was saying.

Dr. Penyu: When we think about infinity it must be the infinite one contemplating itself. Self-consciously wondering what it is like to be. Thinking. So when we think of infinity, that is the self-consciousness of the infinite one.

Steve: Why us?

Dr. Penyu: Because only organisms are capable of self-conscious thought.
Steve: So infinity is self-conscious through us?
Dr. Penyu: Self-consciousness is your resonance with infinity. The self-conscious part of any organism is the part in unity with the infinite one, you see.

Dr. Penyu kept those blue spiral galaxies of silver stars fixed on me.

Dr. Penyu: But you, the whole living human being that makes you, is far removed from unity. Only that tiny, weightless, ethereal bit of you that is your self-consciousness can resonate with unity. Most of the time your consciousness is distracted by navigating the things of the world. In fact, the part of you that manages all that matter and energy cannot be at unity with infinity. Only your overall conscious sense of being one person can resonate with unity.
Steve: Tim and Amy told me that all the energy for thought world comes from me managing my matter and energy. If my unique resonance of thought world and real world is broken, I cease to be.
Dr. Penyu: True. Your ability to be in thought world is dependent on your existence as an organism in real world. Without the mass, energy, organization and vitality of you the human being, your consciousness cannot exist.
Steve: So I have to be alive and conscious to resonate

with infinity, but being a live organism distracts me from my unity with infinity.

Dr. Penyu: That's right.

Steve: The paradox of being.

Dr. Penyu: That's right.

The professor gestured to the largest wall in the pagoda. It was pure white, with no decorations. A floor to ceiling blank white screen.

Dr. Penyu: Well, here it is, my famous projection of what is beyond our cosmic pulse of being.

I looked at the blank white screen, then back to Dr. Penyu. I was perplexed.

Dr. Penyu: Look closely, but please do not touch.

I stepped closer to the pure white wall, expecting to see pixels in the screen, fibers in the paper, or something. But no, it was just pure white. No pixels, no fibers. Nothing.

Steve: Dr. Penyu, I do not see anything.

Dr. Penyu: Are you quite sure?

Steve: Yes, I am sure that all I see is a blank white screen.

Dr. Penyu: That is perfection, you see. I have never understood why people are so fixated on perfection. Perfection is not the point. The point is harmonic resonance.

Steve: Am I supposed to see more?

Dr. Penyu: Do you want to perceive perfection or

harmony?

Steve: Harmony.

Dr. Penyu: Wise choice. Step very close but do not touch. Let the pure light take up your whole field of vision. Look for harmonies.

Steve: How do I find harmonies?

Dr. Penyu: You have an innate, inherited ability to perceive harmonies. Just try.

I tried as hard as I could. I tried to focus on small points, then strained to take in everything at once. I just could not perceive anything beyond blank whiteness.

Steve: I am sorry, but I still just see a blank screen. May I say, I associate harmony with hearing, not sight.

Dr. Penyu: Oh! Amy and Tim did not tell me you are one of those. Okay, let us start with sound. Pay attention to the sonic projection and listen for harmonies. Tell me when you perceive harmonies.

At first there was only soft white noise, a gentle hiss, like the quiet parts of a recording made on magnetic tape. Gradually, almost imperceptibly at first, there were waves lapping against a shoreline. The breaking waves morphed into music. I did not recognize the tune, but it was beautiful.

Steve: I hear music.

Dr. Penyu: Excellent! I have connected with your signal. Look again. I am going to zoom in on individual units of being. Tell me when you see texture.

It took a moment, but sure enough a pattern began to emerge from the pure white.

Steve: Okay, I see something.

Dr. Penyu: What do you see?

Steve: White dots in a three-dimensional lattice within a dark field.

Dr. Penyu: I will zoom in more. Tell me when the dots have texture.

Steve: Now.

Dr. Penyu: Very good. What you have seen so far is frozen in time. I will now project the same lattice greatly accelerated in time. This projection represents how the dots of being in a three-dimensional lattice might look if one could perceive billions of years in a few moments.

The bright spots in the lattice individually glowed and faded, glowed and faded. At times there seemed to be a pattern, at other times not. The glow and fade seemed random.

Dr. Penyu: Can you describe what you see?

Steve: This may sound silly, but can you make the dots orange?

Dr. Penyu: As you wish.

The lattice of glowing and fading orange orbs filled the screen. There were more than I could possibly count.

Dr. Penyu: Now can you describe what you see?

Steve: A boundless crystal of fireflies.

Dr. Penyu: A crystal of fireflies! My, what a lovely metaphor. I have never heard that description. It is so evocative. Not points or dots, but fireflies. Why is that, you think?

Steve: The units of being are alive?

Dr. Penyu: Indeed.

Steve: You mean to say our entire visible universe is a firefly's ass!?

Dr. Penyu, admiring the projection: Not exactly. Our universe is one flash of one firefly's ass. In this model, anyway. Do not forget this is a conjecture.

Steve: So we do not actually exist within one flash of one firefly's ass. That was just to make your story more believable?

Dr. Penyu: It was your metaphor.

Steve: Oh, right. So in your model each flash of each firefly represents an entire universe?

Dr. Penyu: Yes, a cosmic pulse is a universe. Everything you can possibly perceive, including with fancy telescopes, is within one cosmic pulse of being. My projection depicts each of those pulses as a glowing point. A flashing firefly, in your poetic language.

Steve: So our universe is like one bug in an infinite swarm?

Dr. Penyu: Infinity cannot exist without beings. Steve, are you paying attention? What on earth is wrong? Why are you swatting at your face so?
Steve: I'm sorry, Dr. Penyu. I was overwhelmed for a moment with just how unbelievably, incredibly tiny I am. Each glow is a whole universe, with a gazillion galaxies that each have a gazillion solar systems. In my solar system alone there are billions of organisms on Earth like me. Every organism is made of a gazillion cells made of a gazillion atoms. I mean, I'm just nothing, really. Like a single molecule in one cell inside a being made of a gazillion cells.

Tim and Amy ran back in, breathing heavily. They looked flustered and disheveled.
Dr. Penyu: My Tim and Amy, what might you two kids have been doing? Never mind! I do not need to know. Steve here described my model as a crystal of fireflies. Is that not a beautiful and unique metaphor?
Amy, sweaty and catching her breath: Why yes it is.
Tim, panting: Steve does tend to have unusual ideas.
Steve: Hey, I have another idea. I called it a crystal, but what if each glow really is a cell? Maybe each universe is a cell in a huge cosmic brain.
Dr. Penyu: You are forgetting that idea has a limited speed of propagation. If the infinite one was an organism, given the distances between glows, such a mind would

work very slowly indeed.

Steve: Then we must all be in one cell within the mind of a great cosmic turtle!

Tim, Amy, and Dr. Penyu all rolled their eyes at once.

Amy: Steve, you must have gotten that idea from the book that chicken was reading.

Dr. Penyu: It is impossible to know what, if anything, exists beyond our cosmic pulse of being. But I agree that it is exceedingly unlikely that we are in the brain of a cosmic turtle.

Steve: What role do I play, then? I mean, I'm just an insignificant little speck.

Dr. Penyu: You are quite wrong, Steve. First of all, you do not live at the scale I show in my projection. You exist on your scale, as an organism. Only organisms can be self-conscious. Most importantly, you are real. Being real is very special because you are a true harmony of unity, order, variety, idea and stuff.

Steve: But one unit of being like me doesn't matter.

Dr. Penyu: Oh yes, it does. The molecules have to be in harmony for cells to be. The cells have to be in harmony for organisms to be. Organisms must be in harmony for thought to be. Your unit of being is not a molecule. You are an organism that can think.

Tim: As Ambassadors of Thought World, we can imagine

anything we want. But what we imagine is not real.

Amy: You are real, Steve.

Dr. Penyu: And since you are a real organism, Steve, you are very special. You are truly a unique instance of the infinite one. You create thoughts and try to make them real.

Tim: You can drive the harmonies.

Amy: By choice.

Dr. Penyu: Thought world flourishes in organisms like you. I can project an image of harmony as a crystal of fireflies, but it is never more than an image. I cannot put thought into action. Only real organisms like you can think and make choices and act to create real things. That makes you very, very special indeed.

Steve: But I'm still just a little speck. A lot like Ned.

Dr. Penyu: Who's Ned?

Steve: Arak Ned Spinner. A cell in my cerebral cortex.

Dr. Penyu: You named the cells in your cerebral cortex?

Steve: Only that one.

Dr. Penyu: Ah, a chosen one! This Ned must be very special.

Steve: Oh, Ned is special all right. But he was a random choice.

Dr. Penyu: How so?

Steve: Tim and Amy used spider sensors to count the cells in my cerebral cortex. Then they chose one cell at random.

Dr. Penyu, giving Tim and Amy a stern look: Oh they did, did they. Why?

Steve: To make a point.

Dr. Penyu: What point?

Steve: I am not sure I fully understand, but it has to do with the paradox of being.

Amy and Tim said nothing. Tim carefully studied the ceiling to avoid Dr. Penyu's piercing gaze. Dr. Penyu focused her silvery ultramarine blue gaze on Amy. Amy held up both palms and shrugged her shoulders. Dr. Panyu gave them both a long look, then redirected her attention to me.

Dr. Penyu: Knowledge can be so slippery. Your imagination is at unity with the infinite, but the living body that energizes your imagination is quite finite. A tiny speck, if you will. Your speck gives life and order to the trillions of cells that depend upon you to exist. Knowledge of it all is something else again.

Amy: It's the paradox of being, Steve. You are the infinite one, and you are an infinitesimal speck of being.

Tim: All at once.

Steve: I resonate with the infinite one. Infinity is within everything, including me.

Dr. Penyu: Yes, including you. It cannot be any other way. From your perspective, it is not important that you are in the infinite one. What is important is that the infinite one is in you. You are a very special organism adapted to living in a practically infinitely complex environment.

Steve: Why does the infinite one choose complexity over perfection?

Dr. Penyu: Of course we have no way of knowing that. But I have a theory. This is just another guess, mind you. Look at the screen.

The screen resumed being blank.

Dr. Penyu: Here is our image of perfection. Now imagine your thought mirrors how the infinite one thinks.

Steve: I thought it was not possible to know how, or even if, the infinite one thinks.

Dr. Penyu: That is true. We cannot know how or even if infinity thinks. But to help me explain my theory, just pretend for a moment that you and the infinite one think alike. Just pretend.

Steve: Okay.

Dr. Penyu: Now tell me, if you had all eternity to contemplate being, would you rather have this… Dr. Penyu motioned to the blank white screen.

The white screen stayed blank for an uncomfortably long time. Try as I might, I could see no fine structure. I got really tired of looking for something I could not see.

Dr. Penyu, sweeping her arms with a flourish: Or this?

The screen became the lagoon full of life and color. The screen displayed the view of paradise from the old turtle's perspective. It was awesomely beautiful. A riot of colors and forms, all in motion. Beautifully organized infinite waves.

Steve: Given the choice between looking at the variety of beautiful life and staring at a blank screen, I would definitely choose looking at life.

Dr. Penyu: So would I. Tim, Amy?

Tim: Definitely harmony of life over perfection.

Amy: Oh, yes, life is so much more interesting.

Dr. Penyu: And remember, life is always changing. My theory is that the infinite one chooses variety over perfection because variety and change are ever so much more interesting. Which means the infinite one chooses infinite complexity over perfection.

Steve: Chooses? Not chose?

Dr. Penyu: Infinity is now. Always.

Tim: Unity, order, and chaos plus speed limits on idea and stuff create our cosmic pulse of being that evolves toward infinite complexity.

Amy: It is awesome that life in our lagoon all comes from the elegant combination of unity, order, variety, idea and stuff.

Steve: One result of which is me. I am one unique

instance of being within our cosmic pulse of being. My unique instance is one practically infinitely complex organism in a practically infinitely complex environment.

Dr. Penyu, Tim and Amy smiled and nodded to me. Then they all seemed transfixed by the beauty of the lagoon as seen from the old turtle's perspective.

Amanooschence: I had the good sense to give us time to enjoy the moment. But then I could not help myself.

Steve: Your conjecture of real world looked to me like a crystal of fireflies. Do you have a conjecture of thought world?

Dr. Penyu: Yes. It is very speculative. My thought world projection maps imagination. Or perhaps my thought world projection is a map of Earths. I have not yet decided which.

Steve: Please show me.

Dr. Penyu made another sweeping motion before the screen. The lagoon dissolved into an almost inconceivably intricate web. It looked like one tiny portion of a delicate spider web illuminated by a shaft of light, only magnified to completely fill my field of view.

Dr. Penyu: I adored your description of my conjecture of real world as a crystal of fireflies. How might you describe my projection of thought world?

Steve: A close-up of a cobweb illuminated by the sun.

Dr. Penyu: A membrane of life extending like an intricate

spider web in the field of infinite complexity?
Steve: Yes.
Dr. Penyu: Oh, how conventional. But all right. The spiders are such dear souls. Despite that evil cape. I thank you all for visiting! Have a smooth trip home.

The professor lifted two arms straight out to her sides, made a buzzing noise with her lips and started to shuffle hop away.
Steve: Dr. Penyu, may I ask one last question?

Tim and Amy were shocked. Tim seemed embarrassed. Amy was obviously furious. Dr. Penyu stopped buzzing and hopping, slowly lowered her arms to her sides, and gave me a dejected look.
Dr. Penyu, impatiently: If you must.
Steve: Can the infinite one communicate with me directly?
Dr. Penyu: Only in your imagination.

The professor stuck her arms back out, made more lip powered airplane noises, and shuffle hopped in a sweeping curve behind the screen.

Amy stomped out of the pagoda toward Wave Rider. Tim jerked his head in the same direction and shooed me forward with both hands. We walked quickly out of the pagoda, down the verdant path to the dock.
Aminouscious: I wanted to think about how the infinite one could communicate with me through my

imagination. But I could not help but think about how I had disobeyed. I promised Tim and Amy up front that I would not prolong our meeting with Dr. Penyu. I felt bad. I mean, this was my one visit. Tim and Amy would be coming back. Their whole research project must depend on Dr. Penyu's approval. I really had been quite selfish to ask that last question.

As we reached the dock, Amy spun around and got right up in my face.

Steve, under my breath: Uh-oh, here it comes.

Amy: Now you listen to me and listen good.

Steve: Yes, sir, Amy.

Amy, giving me a painfully piercing stare: Are you listening? If you don't listen good I'm going to thwack your ears so hard that F you just earned in obedience school sounds like A sharp pain. You got that?

Steve: Yes, Amy, sir. Please don't thwack me. A sharp from F would hurt real bad.

Amy, yelling: You know what Dr. Penyu was saying about how it doesn't matter how many gazillion beings there are, you're all unique and wonderful and special and precious and all that?

Steve: Um, yeah?

Amy, yelling louder: Well don't you *EVER* forget it!

Amy spun and stalked off toward Wave Rider. Stunned, I looked back to Tim for an explanation. Tim held one finger to his lips and motioned me forward with his other hand. We walked down the dock to Wave Rider. When Tim and I got there, Amy was standing with arms crossed, one knee cocked out and chin held high. Amy was tapping her foot so hard the dock sounded like Tim's bongo drums.

Tim: I'm going to program direct return.

Amy: Whatever.

Tim got into Wave Rider and motioned for me to take my center seat. I did as instructed. Amy pounced in beside me.

Amy: Tim, I'm sorry for being short with you. Direct return is a good idea. Do you want me to prepare turtle brain?

Tim: No, I'll do it. You just relax.

Tim commenced his finger dance across the screen.

Tim: Steve, listen, on the way here we spent great effort to stimulate physical feelings to keep you from getting sick. We are going directly back to our campfire. That means no physical stimulation. I need you to wear the hood the whole time. Trust me, without it you would become violently ill. Sick as in nausea and dizziness that might take practically forever to get over. We don't want that, do we?

Steve: Well, no.

Tim: You will not have to wear the hood for long. But in

addition to no light or sound, this time you will also feel weightless. The complete block of sensory inputs can be very disconcerting. You will intensely feel your body functions. Do not freak out. If you start to feel anxious, just focus on your breathing. Stay calm. You will feel two taps on the tip of your index finger when it is time to take the hood off. Can you handle that?

Steve: Yes, I can handle it. You know, this hood makes me look like a falcon.

Tim: You don't have the beak for it.

Amy, under her breath: Or the brains.

I set the hood in my lap.

Steve: Wait, before we go back, I want to apologize. You told me not to prolong our meeting with Dr. Penyu. But I disobeyed and asked whether the infinite one can communicate with us directly. I am sorry.

Tim and Amy each looked up and away from me. There was an awkward silence. After an uncomfortably long moment Tim cleared his throat.

Tim: Well, Dr. Penyu is usually very understanding. I think everything will be all right.

Amy turned and looked directly into my eyes. She seemed less angry.

Amy: To be perfectly honest, Steve, I have always wanted to ask Dr. Penyu that question.

Steve: Were you surprised by the answer?

Amy: No.
Steve: Tim, how about you, were you surprised that the answer was that the infinite one can only communicate with us in our imaginations?
Tim: No. For me it was like getting the straight scoop on Santa Claus. You might have suspected for a long time that Santa Claus is imaginary. But hearing the truth from an authority you trust and respect gives a certain comforting closure.
Amy: Now put that hood on, and don't be freaking yourself out. We will be back shortly.
Inanewsense: I put the hood on. Exactly as Tim and Amy described, I found myself in a very weird state of having absolutely no external stimuli. I felt like my heart was pounding louder than ever before, even though I was pretty relaxed. I could actually feel the blood flowing through my body. I was breathing normally. But the sound of the air coming in and going out seemed very loud. I realized I move a lot, even sitting still. My nerves glowed and hummed. I thought hey, maybe in this state I can feel my pancreas. I tried really hard to sense it, but honestly I was not even sure where my pancreas was. Try as I might, I had no luck sensing my pancreas. Funny, there's this essential part of me that is vital to my healthy existence. But I cannot feel it, much less consciously control it. My brain must communicate with my pancreas

somehow. I have no clue how. Maybe if I could feel the infinite waves, I could feel my pancreas. I guess if my pancreas hurt, doctors could take images and do tests and explain in detail why I was sick and probably about to die. If that happened, I am sure I would trade most anything to go back to being blissfully ignorant of my pancreas. At times it can be good to be clueless, I guess. So there's this vital part of me that I cannot sense or control. In fact, I would not even be aware of this vital part of me if someone had not told me about it. Makes me wonder what all else is like that.

Interlude Two

Amy, fuming: It's all so unfair. Look at him in that hood. He can be thinking anything he wants. And here we are, Tim, you and me, suspended above oblivion as if by a fragile silk thread.

Tim: I know you are angry, Amy, but please do not punch me in the nose.

Amy: It's not you that makes me angry, Tim. It's the whole deal with this Steve character. Yeah, he had a legitimate question. But the way he crossed Dr. Penyu's boundaries drove home just how powerless we are. Steve could take that hood off, ignore us or forget us, and poof! The silk thread breaks and we disappear into the abyss of eternal nothingness.

Tim: Look on the bright side, Amy. Steve has been paying attention, asking questions, and being engaged. We are in his thoughts, kind of fermenting, in a good way. Despite our rough start.

Amy: Thank goodness for Penyu Tortue's web treatment.

Tim: I know, right? Gentle, subtle, harmless, yet highly effective. Pure genius.

Amy: The depth and breadth of Penyu Tortue's wisdom never ceases to impress me.

Tim: Penyu Tortue's perception is boundless.

Amy: Do you think this Steve character has it in him to absorb Penyu Tortue's whole message?

Tim: I hope so. It's funny. Sometimes Steve is astute, perceptive, and at times almost wise. But at other times he is as dumb as a slug.

Amy: My understanding is that humans are just like that.

Tim: Random organisms are unpredictable, whether slugs or fireflies or humans.

Amy: It still seems really unfair that Steve has so much power over us.

Tim: Well, it's not our job to judge what's fair or not. We were picked to seek harmonies of Penyu Tortue's story with Steve's thoughts. And hey, we are halfway home. Even if our connection breaks, we have already accomplished something.

Amy: We're almost there.

Tim: Want me to lead off Penyu Tortue's theory of knowledge?

Amy: Sure.

6.
Know

Two taps on the tip of my index finger.

I removed the hood and handed it to Tim. We were back in our camp chairs, lined up facing the woods. No sign of Wave Rider. Amy and Tim stood up and walked with their chairs back to their spots by the campfire. I followed their lead and took my own chair back to where I was sitting before.

Tim: Well, Steve, as Ambassadors of Thought World, we have told our story about what it means to be. Are you ready for Penyu Tortue's story of what it means to know?

Steve: Yes, let's do it.

Tim: Excellent. Tell me, Steve, how would you define knowledge?

Steve: Justified belief. To know is to believe for good reason.

Tim: Good reasons to believe what you believe are resonances of thought with being. When your thought is in harmony with an aspect of your reality, you know something.

Amy: Knowledge reflects harmony of idea and stuff.

Steve: I can know because I can resonate with my environment.

Amy: Yes, and since you are a practically infinitely complex wave function in the membrane of life, you can potentially know countless things.
Tim: The membrane of life, which is your environment, is the source of your knowledge.
Steve: Is this where you tell me that all I have to do is truly believe something to make it real? If I can justify a belief, that turns what I believe real?
Amy: No! Absolutely not. The idea that if you can think it up, it becomes real is a delusion. That kind of idealism is fine for science fiction or fantasy or fairy tales. But it is not how beings exist.
Tim: Justified belief does not create your environment.
Amy: But knowledge does help you organize your resonances with your environment. Knowledge can guide your choices of what to select from a gazillion options.
Steve: Just what do you mean by my environment?
Tim: Well, everything outside of you and inside of you.
Amy: You are surrounded by an environment, and within you is a whole environment of billions of cells.
Tim: There's the thought world environment, too, which includes society and all the things people create.
Steve: Including my relationships with family and friends and people I work with. Sounds to me like my environment is basically the field of infinite waves you both keep telling me about.

Amy: Yes, your environment is all the beings and thoughts within and without you.
Steve: Then how can I really know anything?
Tim: Seek order.
Amy: Your nerves create and transmit waves that carry information from your environment.
Tim: You can seek order and make sense of the waves.
Steve: How many waves?
Tim: Gazillions.
Steve: How can I find order and create knowledge from more waves than I can count or comprehend?
Amy: Your perceptions of your environment give you evidence for what resonates with reality.
Tim: You perceive harmonies.
Amy: Then you make selections to create order.
Steve: Should I always try to organize as many perceptions of harmony as possible?
Tim: Only if you can make sense of the perceptions.
Amy: Which can take a long time.
Tim: Maybe even long enough that by the time you make sense of something, it might no longer be real.
Steve: Memories of the past might deceive me in the now.
Amy: Or in the future. Yes, memories might deceive. It depends on whether what you think you know is true.
Steve: How do I know what is true?

Tim: It is. Now, past, future. Is.
Steve: How do I know what is?
Amy: Find resonances.
Tim: Learn the harmonies of unity, order, variety, idea and stuff.
Steve: How?
Amy: Use your imagination. Imagination allows you to navigate the boundless waves from your unique perspective.
Tim: You are. So you must be a harmonic resonance of the boundless waves. Your mind creates an image of itself, your image of you. Your self-image is your self-conception of your resonance in the infinite waves.
Steve: My self-consciousness is my self-image in this moment.
Tim: Yes, your personal picture of your unique resonance.
Amy: You create a unique image of you now. Your self-image is your self-conscious perception of your resonance in the infinite waves.
Tim: Which means you can imagine yourself as a separate being within your environment. That enables you to consciously prioritize the unity, order, variety, idea and stuff surrounding you.
Amy: The harmonies you imagine can include resonances in the past and in the future.

Tim: So you can remember the past and imagine the future.
Amy: You can make choices based on memories and predictions.
Steve: Dr. Penyu told me that I have an innate, inherited ability to perceive harmonies.
Tim: Yes. You can perceive resonances that are invisible in real world, but that reflect reality.
Amy: You know things beyond your unique point in time and space when your imagination resonates with real world.
Tim: But there is a downside to imagination. Your ability to imagine yourself as separate from your environment also means that your self-image in thought world may disconnect from your existence in real world.
Steve: I can be deluded. If my thoughts are not in harmony with my environment, I do not know. I might think I know something, but be wrong.
Tim: It also means that you might know something today that becomes a delusion tomorrow.
Steve: You said I have to be a healthy organism to imagine and navigate.
Amy: Yes.
Steve: So when I die, all my knowledge disappears?
Tim: Yes, when you die your unique imagination ends.
Amy: But your imagination contributes to your

environment.

Tim: You have a legacy.

Steve: But I am only one in a gazillion.

Amy: That doesn't matter. You still count.

Tim: You are a unit of being. You are self-conscious, have a self-image, and can imagine. Therefore you count.

Steve: But I am still only one in a gazillion.

Amy: So true. But infinity has no scale. In thought world, the size of your body makes no difference.

Steve: But Earth is so big.

Tim: Tell me, Steve, do you think Earth is conscious? Aware of itself?

Steve: No. I mean it is the home of conscious organisms like me who can think about what Earth is like. But Earth itself is not conscious.

Tim: And the same is true of stars and galaxies?

Steve: Right. Stars and galaxies are the big environment I live in. People study stars and galaxies and know a lot about them. But stars and galaxies are not conscious. At least I'm pretty sure they are not conscious.

Ammanooscience: To this day I do not know how I would know for sure that galaxies are not conscious. I do not believe galaxies are conscious, but I can't prove it.

Tim: People on Earth know all kinds of things about the Earth and stars. Not to perfection, of course. But humans have figured out a lot about plate tectonics, volcanoes, how the weather works, what kinds of rocks there are, eclipses, novas, things like that.

Amy: You are collectively aware of all kinds of things about Earth and its environment.

Steve: That does not mean Earth is self-conscious.

Tim: Humans live on Earth. Humans are self-consciously aware of Earth.

Amy: So it boils down to how you define self-consciousness.

Tim: But you are right, it makes sense that only organisms with brains can think and remember and imagine.

Amy: Which means whatever the Earth and stars know about themselves is due to the self-conscious organisms like you who live on Earth. That makes you very special.

Tim: Which is the point we have been trying so hard to get across to you.

Steve: So out of a gazillion beings, I am a lucky one to be self-conscious and able to know.

Amy: A truly unique thinking combination of stuff and idea.

Steve: Yet still only one of billions on Earth. I can only know a tiny part of what Earth is really like.

Tim: Relative to your Earth environment, you are very tiny. No denying that.

Steve: Can I transcend being tiny? Can I just live as idea

in thought world?

Amy: No. Idea must resonate with stuff for you to be. Idea alone is nothing. Stuff alone is nothing.

Tim: Take the example of gravity.

Amy: Would gravity exist if there were no units of mass for it to act on?

Tim: What would the idea of gravity be with no stuff to be attracted by it and resonate with it?

Amy: No mass, no gravity. No stuff, no idea.

Steve: So someone has to think about something for it to exist?

Tim: No!

Amy: Absolutely not!

Tim: Steve, part of thought world is just what it sounds like. The world of your thoughts and the thoughts of organisms like you.

Amy: But thought world is more than consciousness. Thought world includes all resonances of order with being, all selections of idea and stuff to create order.

Tim: In the model I projected earlier, thought world is the cone between being and order. Since thought is resonance of order with being, thought world evolves as being evolves.

Amy: Heredity expresses unity. Variation expresses chaos. Selection expresses order.

Tim: Thought world evolves because order among beings

evolves.

Amy: Self-conscious beings like you intentionally make selections and act on them.

Tim: You intentionally create order.

Amy: Creating order makes you a navigator of the boundless waves.

Tim: All beings select from a variety of possible resonances of idea and stuff to create order. Or try to, anyway. If they fail, they perish.

Amy: But most beings do not consciously select among idea and stuff to seek order like you do. Most beings just do whatever comes naturally in their immediate environment.

Tim: But nevertheless the beings make selections by doing things.

Amy: Evolution happens by beings doing things. When a being does something in an environment where there is more than one thing the being might do, that being is making a selection. Selections express order. Most selections are natural consequences that have nothing to do with thinking.

Tim: Selections can be super simple.

Amy: Eating, moving.

Steve: I have never considered what bacteria and amoeba do as thinking.

Tim: It is not thinking, because it is not conscious. But

selection expresses any resonance of order with idea and stuff.

Amy: Bacteria and amoeba and the like all make selections to express order. All successful resonances of idea and stuff express order.

Tim: Thought world is resonance of order with being.

Amy: Selected options that resonate create real world.

Tim: Thought world is the waves. Potential order.

Amy: Real world is the resonances. Realized order.

Steve: So my thinking is one very special instance of thought world.

Amy: Yes, because you self-consciously seek order.

Tim: You actively seek resonances of idea and stuff.

Steve: I get your point that being requires resonance of idea and stuff. But the belief that idea is true reality and beings are but shadows of reality is a very old idea. Lots of people over many years have believed that idea is true reality.

Tim: A lot of people believing something for a long time does not necessarily make the belief correct.

Amy: Idea is not reality. Idea is one aspect of reality.

Tim: Reality is harmonic resonances of unity, order, variety, idea and stuff. Idea by itself is not real.

Amy: People who believe that idea is true reality are correct that reality must include idea. But they are wrong to think idea alone is reality.

Tim: People who believe that matter is true reality are correct that reality must include stuff. But they are wrong to think stuff alone is reality.
Amy: Both idea and stuff are essential. Either by itself is nothingness.
Iminanewsense: This was all beginning to make sense to me. If to be is to be a resonance of unity, order, variety, idea and stuff, it stands to reason that knowledge would be a reflection of that, too. That's how we are. An inherently complex five-way resonance. I had never considered thought as any selection by any being. But it makes sense that selection and order are essential to life.
Steve: All right then, how can I know what resonates with reality and what is delusion? What properly justifies belief?
Tim: People can make what it means to know really complicated. But basically, people have five ways of knowing: instinct, sensation, authority, subjective belief, and logical reasoning.
Amy: No one way of knowing is superior to the others.
Tim: They overlap a lot, and each way of knowing influences the others.
Amy: So do not go tying yourself in knots figuring out whether what you know is by instinct, or sensation, or authority, or subjective belief or logic.
Tim: Shoving things into categories will not help you

know.

Steve: The categories are just a way of organizing my thoughts about thinking.

Tim: Yes. We will start with instinct.

Amy: Instinct is inherited knowledge.

Tim: Instinct is very difficult to identify in people, since you learn so much as you develop.

Amy: You are not at all like a spider that knows how to spin a web without ever seeing it done by another spider.

Tim: For people like you, knowledge you were born with is all mixed up with what you learn.

Amy: You have instincts to feel hungry or thirsty and how to chew and swallow. But you have to learn what to eat and drink, and how to find those good things to eat and drink.

Tim: You also learned how to prepare food. How to prepare food is not instinct, that is learned behavior.

Amy: All the ways people have learned to prepare food took imagination.

Tim: You do have an instinct to imagine.

Steve: People have an imagination instinct?

Amy: Yes. No one has to teach a little kid how to imagine.

Tim: Imagination comes to you by instinct.

Amy: With instinct you just know how to do something. It comes naturally.

Tim: You don't have to think about inherited knowledge.

Steve: So instinct is not really justified belief. There's no belief necessary. No self-conscious awareness, that is.

Amy: True, instinct does not require self-conscious belief.

Steve: So since I don't have to consciously think about what I know by instinct, instinct doesn't really qualify as knowledge.

Tim: True, but only if you strictly define knowledge as justified belief.

Amy: You do not need to justify instinct.

Tim: Instinct is a source of knowledge you cannot survive without.

Amy: Instinct is essential to survival. You might think of instinct as your inner turtle brain.

Tim: It is okay to take your turtle brain for granted.

Amy: Until it growls at you.

Tim: It is not okay to ignore instinct when your inner turtle brain growls at you.

Amy: You need your turtle brain like you need your pancreas.

Steve: Turtle brain growls?

Amy: Not a purr, not a hum, not a sweet harmonic resonance.

Tim: A growl.

Amy: Or a bark maybe.

Tim: Perhaps a hiss.

Amy: A shriek, even.

Tim: When instinct growls or barks or hisses or shrieks or whatever, you have to respond to keep you and your inner turtle brain alive.

Amy: If keeping harmony becomes easy, you can focus your attention on other things.

Tim: Like what the Earth and stars are like.

Amy: But if you are not in harmony with your environment, instinct will warn you.

Tim: And you must respond to survive.

Steve: So what is a growling instinct?

Amy: Hunger.

Tim: Thirst.

Amy: Cold.

Tim: Fatigue.

Amy: When those things growl, you must act. You must do something to resolve the problem.

Steve: Growling instincts become sensations like being cold, hungry, tired, thirsty.

Tim: Yes, those are examples of instincts resonating with sensations.

Amy: Sensations are fundamental to your resonance with your environment.

Steve: By sensation you mean what I can see, hear, taste, smell, and touch.

Tim: Yes. Also pain, hunger, thirst, and feeling cold or hot.
Amy: Sleepy, itchy, feeling like your hair is crawling, queasy, dizzy. All of that.
Steve: So a lot of the same kind of things turtles sense, plus others unique to human me.
Tim: Yes. If you are lucky enough for all your sensors to work well, sensation comes naturally.
Amy: But how to interpret and respond to your human sensations has to be learned.
Tim: You started young and have never stopped learning how to create meaning from sensations and how to respond.
Amy: You work your whole life at learning how to respond to sensations.
Steve: And learning how to justify which sensations are priorities.
Tim: Yes. Given how complex all the sensations you have ever experienced are, it is amazing that you create order and knowledge as well as you do.
Amy: Your mind integrates all your sensations into one unified experience of being you now. Your self-image makes justified belief possible. It's quite marvelous.
Steve: Oh marvelous me.
Tim: There is a tradeoff. You have a single sense of what is real at your unique moment in time. Your self-image

now is your unity.

Amy: But to develop your unity, you have to sense waves that echo reality.

Tim: You exist in your environment's past. Everything you sense is a reflection or echo of reality. There are time lags between waves from your surroundings and your perceptions.

Amy: Plus your body is constantly generating its own waves and chemical signals. The speeds of nerve impulses and chemical processes create time lags, too.

Tim: Which means you can never know for sure whether sensations are from your thoughts, from within your body, or from echoes of reality.

Steve: Marvelous me is a mirage?

Amy: Living in real world tends to keep your sensations and reality aligned. But there is always a fundamental gap between reality and your perceptions of reality, because the waves you sense take time to reach you.

Steve: My sensations of reality are only echoes of real world.

Amy: Yes, echoes. But most of the time your perceptions resonate with reality.

Tim: The time lag between being and perception is usually not significant. At your scale, the speed of light and speed of sound are fast enough to usually be imperceptible.

Amy: Nerve impulses are usually fast enough, too. So the sensations you use to make meaning adequately match the reality you're perceiving.

Tim: If your sensations did not match reality, you would lose the resonance of idea and stuff and weaken or even die.

Steve: My sensations all seem like now to me.

Tim: Your self-image takes the gazillion nerve impulses and turns them into one experience of being you now.

Amy: Your sense of being you now is your self-image, your resonance with unity.

Steve: What if I confuse a sensation from within with a sensation from my external environment? Confuse idea with stuff?

Amy: There's the rub. Something can seem very real to you, but might not resonate with real world.

Tim: A gut feeling might be subjective belief.

Amy: Subjective belief is gut feeling.

Steve: I thought instinct is gut feeling.

Amy: Okay, subjective belief is emotional gut feeling that arises from thinking. It can be self-conscious, but emotions can also arise from subconscious thought.

Tim: Consider instinct as gut feeling from what your body does, and subjective belief as gut feeling from what your mind does.

Amy: Stuff-centered versus idea-centered, if you will.

Steve: Instinct is stuff-centered gut feeling and subjective belief is idea-centered gut feeling.
Amy: That resonates.
Tim: Subjective beliefs include emotions like fear, love, anger. Subjective beliefs can be based on instinct, sensation, imagination, logic, or other beliefs.
Amy: And when you feel confident of a subjective belief, no other information will convince you that what you *know* in your gut is false. No matter how logical their argument might be.
Steve: Like when you're in love.
Tim: Tell us about that, Steve.
Amy: What is it like?
Steve: Being in love is like being at unity with the one you love. When you experience falling in love, there's this overwhelming feeling of oneness. You identify with the loved one and feel intimately connected. Whatever anyone else has to say is pretty irrelevant.
Tim: Is it possible to fall out of love?
Steve: I'm afraid so. The other ways of knowing can definitely cause shifts in subjective belief over time. But being in love is a beautiful feeling.
Amy: So looking back in time, falling in love can look like a delusion?
Steve: It can. But long lasting love is the most valuable experience a person can have. That feeling of unity with

another. Love with unity is precious. So love is worth the risks.

Tim: But it must be tough to never know for sure whether you're delusional or if love will last.

Steve: Are subjective beliefs always delusions?

Tim: No. Subjective beliefs come from the unity in you.

Amy: To know for sure regardless of external evidence is a personal expression of your unique resonance with unity.

Tim: The issue is whether your unique resonance with unity also resonates with your environment.

Steve: When I decide totally on my own what to believe, that is a personal expression of my unity with infinity.

Amy: Yes. A decision to believe and act on your own subjective belief expresses your resonance with unity, your connection with the infinite one.

Tim: Unless you're delusional.

Steve: How can I tell if my subjective belief is true or delusional?

Tim: It's challenging. There is no certain way to tell if a subjective belief is true or delusional.

Amy: Your instincts for self-preservation include protecting your self-image.

Tim: So you have a natural bias to prioritize knowledge from your subjective beliefs. Which makes you prone to self-delusions.

Amy: But if knowledge is genuine, your perceived harmony with unity will also be in harmony with order and variety.
Steve: By genuine knowledge, you mean true harmony of unity, order, and variety?
Amy: Yes. Harmony that resonates with the idea and stuff in you and your environment.
Steve: What do I do if my self-image is not resonating?
Amy: Give us an example.
Steve: Say I have an interesting perspective and I write about it. I feel excited about and proud of my story, so I think everyone should read it.
Amy: So you write it down and put it out there so people can read it.
Tim: They will read it or they won't.
Steve: But maybe hardly anyone reads my story. Maybe the few who do read it do not like it. Maybe people mock me for my story, even. Does that mean my perspective is not interesting?
Amy: It means your writing did not resonate in your social environment.
Steve: That does not really tell me whether my self-image as having an interesting perspective is delusional or not.
Amy: Not directly, but it gives you evidence to consider.
Tim: Feedback from your environment informs your self-image. But it does not dictate it.

Amy: You can still feel good about your story even if what you wrote did not resonate with others.
Tim: Evidence like that from your social environment is an example of knowledge by authority.
Amy: Authority is communal knowledge.
Tim: You can know by being told or shown information from another person.
Steve: Can it be anyone?
Amy: Yes, but for the knowledge to resonate with your environment, your source of information must be trustworthy.
Amy: Knowledge from authority comes from trustworthy sources beyond yourself. It can be in person, by reading a book, seeing it on the internet. Any source outside of yourself.
Steve: What is trustworthy?
Tim: Well, you have to determine that yourself.
Steve: Make my own judgment whether the information resonates with the reality of my environment?
Amy: Yes.
Steve: Is accepting authority a good thing?
Tim: You have to determine that yourself, too. But what others around you believe gives you evidence for what to accept as true.
Amy: To believe and obey authority can bring great peace of mind.

Tim: To accept knowledge from authority spares you the hard work of figuring things out for yourself.
Amy: You can benefit from what others have learned.
Tim: Communal knowledge in harmony with reality can boost resonances in your environment. Resonances in your environment can make your culture more robust.
Steve: More robust?
Amy: Healthy. Have potential to thrive for a long time.
Steve: So trusting authority can increase the health and well being of my culture. Which will increase our legacy.
Tim: If the knowledge from authority is true.
Steve: It is my personal responsibility to distinguish true from false authority.
Tim: Ultimately. If you do not judge for yourself what is true or not, you are a captive of the authority.
Amy: You compromise your free will.
Tim: Which can be good.
Amy: The authority may be wiser than you.
Steve: What if I have reason to believe the authority is not wiser than me?
Amy: Then take full responsibility for yourself and what you believe.
Tim: Even if the current authority contradicts your belief.
Steve: When should I defy authority? No wait stop. You are going to say that is up to me.
Amy: In many cases authority reflects harmonic

resonance. Authority can guide your selections among choices.

Tim: Authority can help you seek harmonies when aspects of your environment are in conflict.

Amy: We need to warn you that trusting yourself to judge whether authority is true or false is much harder than you know.

Tim: It can be very comforting to accept authority, especially when it resonates with your subjective beliefs.

Amy: Plus there can be intense social pressure to accept authority.

Steve: And in the grand scheme of things I don't know much. So I have to rely on the knowledge of others.

Tim: Like we said, any time you trust authority, a great weight of decision-making is lifted.

Amy: Whole swaths of decision making are neatly taken care of. Someone else is responsible. It makes life so much easier. You can think about other things. Especially if your peers insist you must agree their authority is true.

Steve: So unless I want to give up my ability to make my own choices about what to believe, I have to decide which authorities to believe. Let me guess, that's where logical reasoning comes in.

Amy: That's definitely one good use of logic.

Tim: Logical reasoning is the art and science of creating order from what you know from instinct, sensation, emotion, and authority.

Amy: Logic helps you recognize order among your ways of knowing.

Steve: By logical reasoning you mean knowledge based on weighing the best evidence I have.

Tim: Yes.

Steve: The evidence can come from instinct, sensation, emotion, or authority.

Tim: Or logical reasoning.

Amy: The trickiest part of relying on the best evidence to seek order is being aware of what you do not know.

Tim: Right. To find order among sources of knowledge, you must identify where the knowledge came from and determine what knowledge is missing. When you do not know what knowledge is missing, your logic will certainly have errors.

Amy: It is very easy to confuse or neglect sources of knowledge.

Tim: And very difficult to know what you do not know.

Steve: By not knowing you mean thinking one perceives something that is not real, or failing to accept the reality of something that truly is.

Tim: Or being completely oblivious to something.

Steve: Like me and my pancreas.

Amy: Lucky for you, your pancreas knows what to do without you thinking about it. Your pancreas does not

need your logic to function properly.
Tim: Logical reasoning is self-conscious analysis. Your body can run all right without much. Logic is reflective thinking about whether your thought truly reflects order in your environment.
Amy: You are only able to think of a few things at a time.
Tim: There is no possible way to logically analyze everything you encounter in your environment.
Amy: So you have to pick and choose where to apply logical reasoning.
Tim: But if you do not analyze what you think you know, you blunder through life with the self-awareness of a turtle.
Amy: Your inner turtle brain is very adept at instinct, but nearly hopeless at logical reasoning.
Steve: Then how should I choose what to analyze and what to accept as it appears to be? How do I decide when to use my logical human brain and when to rely on my instinctive turtle brain?
Amy: That is totally up to you.
Steve: Grrr. Okay, I knew that. But what if I misidentify the relevant ideas and stuff? I mean, you made it clear that I sense echoes of reality. There's no objective way to know if my perceptions are true resonances with reality.
Tim: You are correct. Knowledge is never one hundred percent certain. Complete truth is unattainable.

Amy: The closer you get to harmony, though, the greater your being.
Tim: Logic helps you decide which evidence from your environment is worth acting on.
Amy: If you apply justified belief wisely through your choices and actions, logic can help you increase harmony. Increase harmony, increase your legacy.
Tim: Logic or critical thinking or whatever you want to call analytical thought is a great tool for finding harmonies in your complex environment. The greater your harmony, the greater your being and legacy.
Amy: Your harmony is your legacy.
Steve: It's all about maximizing harmony within my practically infinitely complex environment.
Amy: That's right. Resonate.
Tim: Lucky for you, humans have figured out what a useful tool logic can be to find harmonies.
Steve: Harmonies as in turning ideas from thought world into things in real world.
Tim: You got it.
Amy: In your own bumbling, error-prone way, people have become quite good at finding order amongst ideas and things.
Tim: A key to what has made humans so good at making thought world real has been your discovery of the waves around and within you.

Amy: People have made incredible advances by figuring out how to perceive and control waves.

Tim: Just look at all the ways people perceive and control waves: music, radio, electricity, internet, microwaves, X-rays, ultrasound, tomography. The list goes on and on. Every way people communicate with one another relies on waves. The stuff part of the infinite waves.

Amy: People have also become quite creative by figuring out how to model waves. Calculus, statistics, economics. Things like that. The idea part of the infinite waves.

Tim: People are really good at turning thoughts into reality by finding harmonies of idea waves and stuff waves.

Amy: Real things like songs, paintings, films, sculptures, comic books, bridges, buildings, roller coasters, tents, chairs.

Tim: When you turn a thought into a real thing, the thought becomes more likely to be remembered by future generations of people. Realized thoughts become stuff legacies.

Amy: Humans are becoming scary good at turning images into real things and turning real things into images. The boundaries between what is thought and what is real are becoming quite fuzzy. It is so easy to play tricks with what is idea and what is stuff.

Tim, looking like he'd just lost his queen in a big chess

match: People used to have to use your hands to make things.

Amy: But now other tools have greatly expanded creativity beyond what hands can do.

Tim: Hands are really remarkable.

Steve: What remark would you make about hands?

Amy: Should I sing the hand song?

Tim, excited: Yes! Go for it, girl!

Amy stood up, laced her fingers with palms facing me, cracked her knuckles, then flourished her fingers like a flamboyant magician preparing to pull a rabbit from a hat.

Steve, over his shoulder: Birds and mammals, sound alert!

Amy held her hands out toward me and sang in a sweet contralto:

Unity is in your pinkie
Order wears a ring
Chaos gets the middle finger
'Cause variety is its thing
Idea is in your index finger
Stuff is in your thumb
Work them all together and
What can then become?
Anything your mind can think of
If it can be done.

Amy's fingers danced to the tune, each finger playing its role in turn. She made big question marks at "what can then become?" and sprayed me with imaginary dust at "*If* it can be done."

Tim leapt up: Bravo! Bravo! Tell me Steve, is that not the best song ever?

Steve, laughing: It's good, I like it. Your song is a handy way to show how unity, order, variety, idea, and stuff can be so creative.

Amy, with a bow: Thank you.

Amy sat down and smiled. A mockingbird sang a lovely version of the hand song. Crickets chirped and frogs croaked. It was a happy moment for us all.

Steve: So is there a song for knowing?

Tim: Why don't you give it a try, Steve?

Amy: Yes, you please sing a knowledge version of the hand song for us.

Steve: Well, I am not sure. I'm not much of a singer.

Amy: You will do fine.

Tim: Yes, Steve, give it a go.

Steve: Singing is not really my thing, and neither is improvisation, but I feel inspired by that mockingbird. I'll try.

I stood up, held out my hands like Amy had, and sang:

Instinct is in my pinkie
Sensations have a ring
Subjective belief gets the middle finger
'Cause variety is its thing
Authority points my index finger
Logic guides my thumb
Work them all together and
What can then become?
Anything I can think of
If it can be done.

Amy and Tim clapped their hands.

Tim: Well done!

Amy: I love it!

Tim, with a sigh: Sad thing is, you cannot be in perfect harmony. Your mind and hands cannot do everything.

Amy: Tim, you can be such a killjoy. But Tim is correct. As a being, you cannot attain perfect harmony of unity, order, and variety.

Steve: I can be better, but I can never be perfect.

Amy: Being perfect is not the point. Ability to navigate the boundless harmonies is the point.

Steve: The better I can navigate the boundless harmonies, the greater my being and legacy.

Amanewcents: I stared into the fire for a minute, taking this in the best I could. As psychological experiments go, this was one heck of a treatment. By this point I had totally lost any sense of what Tim and Amy might be measuring about my reaction to this whole Ambassador of Thought World routine. I had also ceased to care.

Steve: So, okay. I can accept that it's not about perfection. It's about infinite complexity and boundless harmonies. Knowledge helps me navigate. But infinity is not a being. You made that clear when you mocked me for my idea that we are a cell inside the brain of a cosmic turtle.

Tim: That's right. Infinity is there, but it is not a being.

Steve: You call me a unique instance of the infinite one. That means I am a being within infinity. Which can only be because infinity is. I exist because infinity exists.

Amy: Yes. There is only one infinity, the unity of all. You are part of it.

Tim: So what you think must somehow be part of the infinite waves.

Steve: Since infinity has no time or scale, infinity is unity, always everywhere at once, including in me.

Amy: And you are self-consciously aware of infinity.

Tim: Which makes you an instance of the self-consciousness of the infinite one.

I thought of Dr. Penyu.

7.
Remember

Amy: Dr. Penyu, you startled me.

Dr. Penyu: How?

Amy: I did not expect to see you here.

We were all startled. All of a sudden Dr. Penyu was sitting next to us by the fire. She sat cross-legged with her spine erect. Her attractive hands held a red wool blanket around her shoulders. Dr. Penyu's luxurious white hair framed her mature beauty.

Steve: How did you get here, Dr. Penyu?

Dr. Penyu: How?

Tim: Yes, how?

Amy: I want to know, too.

Dr. Penyu: I got in the back of Wave Rider while you were philosophizing about Santa Claus and covered myself with this red wool blanket.

Steve: Have you been sitting here the whole time? I did not notice you.

Dr. Penyu: No. I was over admiring the fireflies. They are quite tame, actually. Almost silent, too. Which surprised me. I asked them to fly in a crystalline lattice formation, but they ignored me. Beasts.

Steve: My understanding is fireflies naturally fly in

random swarms.

Dr. Penyu: So it would appear.

We all quietly sat by the campfire for one hundred and thirty-seven seconds. Give or take a bit.

Dr. Penyu: I came along because I would very much like to meet Arak Ned Spinner.

Steve: Meet crazy Ned? Why?

Dr. Penyu: Your imagination is your unique resonance with the infinite one. So your imagination is potentially infinite. But your imagination relies on self-conscious thought. Self-conscious thought relies on a healthy brain. A healthy brain can only exist within a healthy organism. Within your healthy organism there must be many healthy cells. I have never considered all of this from the perspective of one of the gazillion cells in your brain. This seemed to me a good opportunity to get a fresh perspective.

Steve: So an organism like me is special because I have a brain that can imagine due to the lives of a gazillion cells.

Amy: Which means you can live in thought world.

Tim: And Ned the cerebral cortex cell is part of what makes your existence in thought world possible.

Steve: I can think and imagine because I include a gazillion Neds.

Dr. Penyu: So, Tim and Amy, could you kindly connect us with Ned?

Iamanusciance: I pictured Ned thrashing back and forth and spouting nonsense.
Steve: Wait! I am not sure I am up for this. Ned can be very, well, excitable.
Dr. Penyu: Well of course. It is the nature of a neuron to be excitable.
Amy: It will be okay, Steve.
Tim: Dr. Penyu shared her projection.
Amy: Now it's your turn.
Tim: Amy's right. Just trust Dr. Penyu.
Steve: This has been one heck of a roller coaster ride. So far, the rewards have been worth the risks. So all right. I'll do my part. Connect with Ned.
Tim: Steve, when we connect with Ned, you do the talking, at least at first.
Steve: Why?
Amy: That is what Ned will be expecting. He'll feel hurt if you don't.
Steve, reluctantly: Okay.

Tim made a sweeping motion from his sleeve. The screen appeared as before. The screen brightened. There was Ned, same as before. Tim nodded to me. Dr. Penyu beamed a big goofy grin.

Steve: Hello, Ned.
Ned, startled: Just Steve?!?
Steve: Yes, just Steve.

Ned, in fear: Are you here to smite me?

Steve: No, Ned, of course not. I am not here to smite you.

Ned: I thought you had abandoned me. You left as I sought to honor you.

Steve: Yes, well, sorry about that. I had other things I wanted to attend to.

Ned, shivering: So you are not back to get revenge and apoptose me?

Steve: No, Ned. I would like to talk with you some more.

Ned: That is well, oh Just Steve, as you left me with more questions than answers.

Steve: I cannot promise that you will not feel that way again, Ned. There are always more questions than answers. But we want to get to know you better. Do you remember Amy and Tim?

Ned: The Ambassadors of Thought World?

Steve: Yes.

Ned: Of course. Hello, Tim.

Tim: Hi Ned.

Ned. Hello, Amy.

Amy: Hello, Ned. How are you?

Ned: Not smitten.

Amy: Is that a good thing?

Ned: Oh yes indeed. With Just Steve's indulgence I live another day. I greatly feared that Just Steve would smite me.

Steve: Ned, I promise not to smite you, okay? I could not smite you even if I wanted to. At least not without smiting myself, too.

Ned, quaking: Okay.

Steve: We have someone else with us this time. I would like to introduce Dr. Penyu.

Ned, apprehensively: What sort of a doctor is Dr. Penyu? Not a neurosurgeon, I hope.

I did not know what sort of doctor Dr. Penyu might be. I patiently waited for one of my companions to reply. It had something to do with math. Which is like saying water has something to do with life. A doctor of anything has to know some math, one would think. Tim fiddled with his palm. Amy looked about on the ground, as if checking to make sure no slugs were sneaking up on her. Dr. Penyu gazed impassively into the campfire. It appeared to be up to me to identify what sort of doctor Dr. Penyu was.

Steve: Dr. Penyu is a doctor of psychology.

Dr. Penyu: Nice call.

Ned: So Dr. Penyu, you are a doctor of psychology?

Dr. Penyu: Yes.

Ned: You are here as a professional companion for Just Steve as he talks with one of the cells in his brain?

Dr. Penyu: That's right.

Ned: Um, tell me, Dr. Penyu, doctor of psychology, is

Just Steve maybe a little bit, you know, well . . ..

Ned curled an axon inward and twirled one of its finger-like terminals in circles around where Ned's head would be. That is if Ned had a head.

Dr. Penyu: Oh, no, Steve appears to be quite competent at being just Steve. I do not think he is crazy.

Ned: So Just Steve is not going to go bonkers and smite me?

Dr. Penyu: I consider it exceedingly unlikely that Steve will go bonkers and smite you.

Steve: Ned, I am not going to smite you or apoptose you or draw and quarter you or anything like that. I promise. Please relax.

Tim, squeamishly: Draw and quarter?

Steve: I promise. Relax.

Ned: I shall try. But tell me, how am I the chosen one?

Tim: It was random.

Ned: How?

Tim: We counted all the cells in Steve's cerebral cortex and chose one at random.

Dr. Penyu coughed and adjusted the blanket around her shoulders.

Ned: So I am the lucky winner of a one in a gazillion lottery.

Tim: Correct.

Ned: I'm not special, just lucky.

Amy: Being lucky is being special. One in a gazillion.

Ned: How many is a gazillion?

Tim: More than you can count.

Amy: More than you can comprehend.

Dr. Penyu: Ned, whether you are special or lucky, you are unique. We want to talk with you. Will you please talk with us?

Ned: Yeah, okay. But first let me get this straight. You are saying I am a cell like countless others. I am only one of a gazillion?

Dr. Penyu: Yes. But you have the lucky specialty of being a cerebral cortex cell within Steve.

Ned: To make extra sure I understand this correctly, what is a cerebral cortex?

Dr. Penyu: The part of Steve's brain that thinks.

Ned: And a brain is what?

Dr. Penyu: The part of Steve that manages his organism.

Ned: And an organism is?

Dr. Penyu: A living being that finds ways to survive in its environment.

Ned: And the environment is?

Dr. Penyu: In Steve's case, the surface of the planet Earth.

Ned: Just Steve's environment is Earth?

Dr. Penyu: Yes.

Ned: So Just Steve is an organism that lives on Earth like

I am a cell that lives in Just Steve's brain.
Dr. Penyu: That's right. You are very lucky to be in Steve's brain.
Amy: Ned, if you were not a cell in Steve's cerebral cortex, you could have been a microbe anywhere on Earth.
Tim: Maybe in the guts of a slug.

Amy gave Tim an angry frown and hunched her muscular shoulders.
Amy, threateningly: Tim, if you don't cut it out, I am going to use my two hands to squish your brains like a slug between two flat rocks.
Tim: Ew.

Tim stuck his index fingers out from beside his eyeballs and pretended to be a slug looking around. The tips of his index finger slug eyes slowly twirled side to side and up and down.
Amy, studiously ignoring Tim: Ned, you are lucky to be in Steve instead of inside a slug or out in the dirt.
Ned: How so?

Tim's waving fingertip eye stalks gave Ned a good looking over as he spoke.
Tim: Well, if you were a cell out on its own, you would have to fend with finding food and staying warm. If you were inside of a slug, well, you would be inside of a slug.
Amy: Ned, I will try to improve on slug brain's

explanation.

Tim continued waving around his finger eyes and tried to contort his mouth to look like a slug. He wasn't very convincing.

Amy: Inside Steve's brain where you live, all the food gets delivered, waste pickup is free, and the temperature is kept remarkably constant. As long as Steve stays healthy, you are on easy street. Everything you need is taken care of.

Tim: Plus you have the chance to live a really long time, as cells go. Definitely better than being inside a slug.

Tim withdrew his slug eyestalks and put them in his lap.

Amy: Ned, you landed quite a good deal being a neuron in Steve's cerebral cortex.

Ned: So when I process the nerve impulses, I'm Just Steve's thoughts?

Dr. Penyu: Yes, you contribute to Steve's thoughts.

Ned: So I control Just Steve's thoughts?

Dr. Penyu: No. Your actions combine with many others to create Steve's thoughts. Your one contribution has but little influence on the whole. You see, Ned, the nerve impulses you process resonate with many others to create potential thoughts.

Ned: How many others?

Dr. Penyu: A gazillion others. How potential thoughts

become real is up to Steve.

Steve: If I understand this correctly, when enough neurons like you send resonant signals, those signals become my thoughts. If I pick them.

Ned: So I am an infinitesimally small cell that has a tiny chance to influence Just Steve's thoughts. Oh lucky me.

Amy: Yes, but you are important nevertheless.

Steve: I cannot think without you. Or others like you.

Ned: You pick from me and a gazillion others.

Steve: Yeah, so?

Ned: I am not important if I am expendable.

Steve: Yes you are. I need you.

Ned: I'm just one in a gazillion!

Steve: That doesn't matter, Ned. I still need you. I have to pick from lots of cells like you to think.

Dr. Penyu: Ned, could you explain for me what it is you do with the nerve impulses you process?

Ned: Well I have to tell the truth. Before Amy and Tim and Just Steve visited me, I never thought about it. I never thought about anything, actually. This thinking thing is all very new to me.

Amy: I must say, Ned, you are handling it very nicely.

Ned: Thanks for the boost. If you want something of me, I need a boost. Boosting and shutting down signals is what I do. It's by instinct, really.

Dr. Penyu: What kind of signals boost you?

Ned: There are two types, but they always work together. One type of signal comes from waves of electricity. The other type of signal comes from waves of chemicals. When the waves of electricity and the waves of chemicals resonate, they create flavors.
Dr. Penyu: Flavors?
Ned: I do not know how else to describe what I choose to boost. Some resonances of electricity and chemicals taste really good. I boost those along their way. Some taste so good they give me a boost. Many impulses are a combination of electricity and chemicals that are not especially flavorful one way or another. I just let those on through. But sometimes combinations of waves and chemicals taste really nasty. I inhibit the nasty flavors the best I can. Spit them right out.
Dr. Penyu: How do you shut down the bad flavors?
Ned: I simply do not replicate the wave. If I don't keep the wave going, it stops.
Dr. Penyu: How do you replicate waves that taste good?
Ned: I control the electricity. I have to admit I am not really sure how. I just do it by instinct.
Dr. Penyu: Interesting. Now, Ned, you know that inside of you are numerous structures.
Ned: Like the organelles I was trying to kill when I thought self-sacrifice was what Just Steve wanted of me?
Dr. Penyu: Yes. Which organelles were you trying to

sacrifice?
Ned: Well, at that moment I was straining to kill some mitochondria.
Dr. Penyu: Did you kill any?
Ned: No. Just Steve stopped me. He told me that sacrificing organelles was not helpful. So of course I stopped. Truth is though, I was not having any luck killing them. I found that simply thinking about killing parts of myself made no difference. My effort did have a fragrant unintended consequence, though.
Dr. Penyu: Stinky unintended consequences can happen to the best of us. As you know, Ned, in addition to mitochondria, you have many structures within you that perform specific functions. Some process food energy, some pump ions, some carry waste away. Ned, you are in fact an amazingly complex cell.
Ned: How flattering. Are you flirting with me, Dr. Penyu?
Dr. Penyu: No. I simply want to point out that you are practically infinitely complex.
Ned: Although I am still only one in a gazillion.
Dr. Penyu: Being one in a gazillion doesn't make you any less of a marvel of evolution.
Ned: So then what are the other gazillion cells in Just Steve doing?
Dr. Penyu: Well, like we said, you are inside the part of Steve's brain that thinks. Other parts of Steve's brain

control the many processes it takes to eat, move energy around, breathe, keep the temperature right, and many other things.

Ned: Sounds complicated.

Dr. Penyu: Oh, it is. The process of keeping Steve alive and healthy is a gazillion complex.

Ned: Just Steve, how do you keep track of it all?

Steve: Lucky for me, most of the gazillion complex processes go on without me thinking about them.

Ned: Like how I process waves without thinking about them.

Steve: That's right. You know what to do without me having to explain it to you. I know what to do without others having to explain to me what to do. Sort of.

Dr. Penyu: Ned, for how you help Steve think, I would like to talk about your impulses. Nerve impulses happen when positive charges rush across your membrane. That causes little lightning bolts of energy inside you. Those lightning bolts are part of the stuff of your existence. They cause the waves that contribute to Steve's thoughts.

Ned: The rush of positively charged ions are part of my stuff.

Dr. Penyu: Yes, the lightning bolts go through you in waves.

Ned: I have some control over those waves.

Dr. Penyu: Yes, the waves of impulses carry information.

The waves are part of the idea of your existence.

Ned: The flavors are the ideas.

Dr. Penyu: Right. In the overall big picture, what you do is transport ideas through the flavors of the waves. The ideas you transport contribute to Steve's thoughts.

Ned: The waves are idea. The lightning bolts are stuff.

Dr. Penyu: You see how idea and stuff are connected within you?

Ned: Yes, idea and stuff resonate in the waves I process.

Dr. Penyu: Exactly. Now, as we were saying before, you are a very complex cell that processes stuff and idea. You keep those ionized molecules in the right places at the right times. Then by instinct you process lightning bolts and transmit waves. All that takes a lot of energy. You get that energy from the food Steve eats. The food gets processed by various parts of his body that turn it into forms that you can use.

Ned: Just Steve feeds me.

Dr. Penyu: Yes. Steve feeds your mitochondria and the waves and everything else in you.

Steve: Ned, you are one piece of the various parts that all together make me. You are filled with variety and surrounded by variety.

Ned: All those parts and waves are my variety.

Dr. Penyu: Yes, and they resonate with your stuff and idea. But all that variety in you would just be chaos if there were no order. Your choices help create order in Steve.

Tim: Order you create by what you select to do helps keep all of Steve's parts working together as one.

Amy: The main source of order in you, Ned, is the DNA in your nucleus.

Tim: DNA codes tell the various parts in you how to select among options.

Ned: The DNA in my nucleus provides order.

Dr. Penyu: Yes, but some of your order comes from the nature of all the molecules that are part of your amazing variety. For example, your DNA does not have to tell positive ions to be attracted to negative ions. That order is part of their nature.

Ned: So within my variety and order, there are more layers of variety and order.

Dr. Penyu: Precisely. The same is true of layers outside of you. In fact, the DNA inside you is the same as the DNA inside all the other cells in Steve.

Ned: All of them?

Dr. Penyu: Well, almost all. Some blood cells have no DNA, and there are many cells within Steve that live in him as guests. But that is a quibble. Your DNA is the same as the DNA throughout Steve. The code for your order is the code for Steve's order.

Ned: Just Steve and I share the same code for order?

Dr. Penyu: That's right.

Ned: My order is Just Steve's order. Imagine that. We are the same.

Dr. Penyu: In terms of DNA that encodes order, yes, you are the same.

Ned: Does that mean I am a very small version of Just Steve?

Dr. Penyu: Not really, because the scale of Steve's variety, stuff, and idea are different from your scale. You are a cell. Steve is an organism.

Ned: Oh, right, I am one in a gazillion.

Dr. Penyu: But you are one. You are unique. It is true there are many cells like you. But you are the one and only Arak Ned Spinner. Your unity resonates with your order, variety, stuff, and idea.

Ned: Being me is my unity.

Dr. Penyu: Yes. Being you is being your unique resonance of unity, order, variety, stuff, and idea.

Ned: So Just Steve has a giant DNA code like a gazillion times bigger than mine?

Tim: Ned, actually all of the DNA code is copied in each individual cell. All of Steve's DNA is just like the DNA in your nucleus.

Ned: There is no one master all-knowing DNA code?

Tim: Yes and no. The code is the same throughout Steve. But each copy of DNA code is a unique instance within each of the forty trillion cells of Steve's body. There is no one big code that dominates the others. Each copy of DNA is in the nucleus of each cell. All forty trillion of them. Including you.

Ned: How can that be?

Tim: Well, Steve started out as a fertilized egg. An egg from his mother combined with a sperm from his father to form one unique DNA code. Half came from the mother, and half from the father.

Ned: Just Steve started as a single cell with one DNA code?

Tim: That's right.

Ned: Just like me?

Tim: Yes, Steve started out as one unique cell just like you. In that way you and Steve are the same.

Amy: You have the same DNA.

Ned: How did one cell like me become a gazillion and develop into Just Steve?

Tim: Well, the fertilized egg that Steve started out as divided into two cells, then four, then sixteen, and so on. The cells just kept growing and dividing until they became Steve.

Ned: And I am one of those cells?

Tim: Yes.

Ned, in awe: Just Steve is a big blob of a gazillion cells just like me.

Dr. Penyu: Ned, the cells in Steve all have the same DNA, but each cell has a special job to keep Steve alive.
Ned: I am really confused.
Dr. Penyu: It is easy to understand how you might be confused. Every cell in Steve contains the code for Steve, and the code for being an individual cell in Steve.
Amy: Ned, there is the whole code, and there is the code relevant to what each cell needs. As Ned, you use the Ned portion of the DNA code. There sort of is a giant DNA, but the whole code is in every cell, including you. You prioritize the parts of the code that you need to be Ned. Ned selects the parts Ned needs to maintain order and be Ned.
Tim: Other cells select whatever parts of the code they need to create order and be their unique selves.
Ned: Aren't you all making this way more complicated than it needs to be? I mean, Just Steve simply makes all this happen, right?
Steve: How do you mean, Ned?
Ned: Great all-knowing Just Steve, you created all the cells in you and you guide them and nurture them.
Steve: Well in some ways I do, I guess, in the sense that when I eat and keep myself warm I keep everything going. But Dr. Penyu, Tim, and Amy are correct. Most of what happens in me happens without me knowing much of anything about it. I am not aware of the cell codes.

Ned: How can that be, oh great Just Steve?

Steve: The part of me that thinks and is aware of my environment is only a small portion of everything I am. Most of what keeps all the cells like you alive and well happens without me ever having to think about it.

Ned: You mean if you had not picked me at random, you would have never even been aware of my existence?

Steve: Yes, to be honest.

Ned: Well you have to be honest, right?

Steve: Yes, Ned, I have to be honest.

Ned: Be honest. Will you remember me?

Steve: Yes, Ned. I can assure you that I will remember you.

Dr. Penyu: We would all like to be remembered. That is how anyone lives in thought world.

Amy: Being remembered is to be in thought world.

Tim: In thought world, to be is to be remembered.

Ned: I will remember you, too, Just Steve. Wonderful Just Steve, may I most humbly ask a simple question of you?

Steve: Yes, Ned.

Ned: If you are a random being within infinity, who picked you?

Steve: What do you mean, who picked me?

Ned: You said that Tim, Amy and you randomly picked me. So who picked you?

Steve: No one picked me. I just am.

Ned: But you can think, right?

Steve: Yes.

Ned: So if you are a being that can think, that means you won a one in a gazillion lottery. It must take gazillions of idea waves resonating with gazillions of stuff waves to create a thinking organism as complex as you. You must be one in a gazillion.

Steve: Right along with billions of my peers.

Ned: Like I am one brain cell among a gazillion. You picked me. Who picked you?

Steve: Well, I had parents that created me and helped me grow and learn.

Tim: If I may interject…

Steve: Please do!

Tim: I think, Ned, that Steve took your question in a different context from what you may have intended. One could say that Amy and I, Ambassadors of Thought World, picked Steve.

Ned: And then you all together picked me.

Tim: That's right.

Ned: Well, since we are all together chosen ones, I have another question. So Just Steve, when you aren't talking with me, Arak Ned Spinner, are you staring into nothingness? Like a neuron without a signal to process?

Steve: No, far from it. I perceive and think about many

things.

Ned: How do you make sense of it all?

Steve: I don't know. It comes naturally. Most of the time. Sometimes I sense things that I do not understand and cannot make sense of.

Ned: What do you do then?

Steve: Well, either I choose to ignore the sensation or thought, or I try to find order to create meaning.

Ned: Were you born knowing how to make meaning from sensations and thoughts?

Steve: Oh, no, it takes years to learn to make sense of it all.

Ned: So how does Just Steve choose what to think about?

Steve: Much of the time I think about how to adapt to what is going on around me. That is thinking in the now. But I can also remember things that happened in the past and wonder about things that may happen in the future.

Ned: Yes, but from all those choices in the past, present, and future, how do you select what to think about?

Steve: It can be pretty random.

Tim: Like a chicken reading a book.

Ned: What?

Amy: Like a chicken reading a book.

Ned: You lost me.

Steve: Oh, when we were riding the idea waves on our visit to Dr. Penyu, I imagined that I saw a chicken reading a book.

Ned: What book was the chicken reading?

Steve: *Flags Up!* by Lillian Mountweazel.

Ned: Never heard of it.

Tim: Ned, have you ever read any book?

Ned: Well, no.

Steve: That would explain why you have not heard of it.

Ned: What is this book about?

Steve: Actually, it is an imaginary book by an imaginary author.

Ned: So you thought about an imaginary chicken reading an imaginary book by an imaginary author.

Dr. Penyu: All has an elegant symmetry to it, actually.

Amy: So you made up that author, Steve?

Steve: No, I did not make up the author.

Tim, pressing his glasses up and scrunching his nose: Who made up the author, then?

Steve: Look, the story is not worth telling.

Ned: Are you keeping secrets from us, Just Steve?

Steve: No! Who made up the author is simply not that interesting of a story. I do not want to bore you.

Amy: Try us. We love a good story.

Steve: It is not that good.

Ned: Please.

Steve: Okay, I will try to keep the author story brief. Back before the internet, if you wanted to look up a fact about something, you read about it in a printed book. Businesses published fact-filled books called encyclopedias. Publishers put a lot of time and money into making these fact books. It was big business. But it took a whole lot of work. Untrustworthy publishers sometimes stole content from others to save time and money.

Tim yawned.

Steve: So once upon a time one of these encyclopedia publishers decided to create a trap. They made up a fake entry for Lillian Virginia Mountweazel. She never existed.

Amy: Except in the encyclopedia entry.

Steve: Right. But she was not real. So if some other publisher included the story about Mountweazel, it would be obvious that the content was stolen. Because Lillian Virgina Mountweazel was never real.

Tim: So where does *Flags Up!* come in?

Steve: It was part of the encyclopedia entry. Lillian had published a photo essay of mailboxes titled *Flags Up!*

Amy: What became of Lillian?

Steve: She got accidentally blown up while on photo assignment for *Combustibles* magazine.

Amy: Oh, how awful. I hope she did not have any children.

Ned: Which crazy neurons allowed you to combine your

memory of that with an imaginary chicken?
Steve: Like I said, what I think about can be pretty random.
Tim: I'll say.
Dr. Penyu: There is a very important lesson in Steve's story about the chicken reading this imaginary book.

Silence. Dr. Penyu looked serenely into the campfire. We all waited expectantly to hear what Dr. Penyu had to say. How might there be an important lesson in my imaginary chicken story?
Dr. Penyu: The infinite one leaves beings free will so that infinite complexity can come to be. The world around us has boundless harmonies. But in theory, there is a count of things. There are a gazillion beings. More than anyone can count or comprehend. But in theory there are not actually an infinite number of beings. In theory, the infinite one could count the beings. But when you have beings that can imagine, there are no limits. The infinite one cannot count what might be imagined. Steve's image of an imaginary chicken reading an imaginary book by an imaginary author is one example of how imagination is boundless. The infinite one is truly infinite because of beings with imaginations.
Ned, awestruck in the moonlight: My processing of the waves contributes to the infinite one's imagination, too.
Dr. Penyu: That is correct, Ned.

Ned: So Just Steve, do you feel like you control the infinite one?
Steve: Oh, heavens no. I contribute just the tiniest little bit, if anything at all. Heck, I don't really even control me. At least in some ways I do not control me.
Ned: I do not understand, Oh great Just Steve.
Steve: Ned, before, when you were going on about all the wonderful things I do for you, one of the things you called me was Giver of Glucose. Do you remember that?
Ned: Yes, Just Steve, you are the Great Giver of Glucose, oh marvelous one!
Steve: Well, in a way I am the Giver of Glucose, because I eat food. I have to eat to live. I do have a lot of control over what I find to eat, how I prepare it, and how much I consume.
Ned: You are most powerful, Just Steve, Great Giver of Glucose!
Steve: Not so much, Ned. You see, once I have eaten the food, my body takes care of breaking it down into the glucose and everything else you and all the other gazillion cells in me need.
Ned: You do not control that?
Steve: Not in my thoughts, anyway. In fact, there is this part of me called the pancreas that plays a vital role in the whole glucose thing.
Ned: How does Just Steve control this pancreas?

Steve: I don't. I mean not consciously, anyway. I suppose my brain communicates with my pancreas somehow, but I am not aware of it.
Ned: So you cannot say, "Pancreas, make some more glucose for Ned."
Steve: I can say those words, but it would have zero effect on my pancreas, glucose levels, or you. To be honest, Ned, the vast majority of everything that goes on in my body goes on without me knowing anything about it.
Ned: Just Steve is not all-knowing.
Steve: Just Steve does not know much. Even about myself.
Ned: I feel let down.
Steve: Me, too.
Dr. Penyu: You are both being too negative. It is true that you cannot know much, at least relative to all there is to know. But nevertheless you are both one in a gazillion beings. You are very lucky to be exactly who you are.
Ned: Just Steve, I have trouble believing you cannot control half of what goes on in your body. You mean to say that you are the master of my existence but don't know half of what is going on?

Tim loudly cleared his throat.

Steve: What I consciously control is much less than half.
Ned: How much less than half?

Steve: I do not know. I have no way of knowing that.
Ned, deflated: You do not even control your own existence? Much less mine?
Steve: Well, yes and no. I eat, I breathe. I live. I do think about what I eat. I kinda sorta think about how I breathe. All that keeps us going. I don't think much about living, except for realizing I will not live forever.
Ned: Tell me this, Just Steve. Can you think yourself dead? Apoptose yourself?
Steve: Just by thinking? No.
Ned: So you cannot think yourself dead. Null. Nothing. A. Pop. Tosed.
Steve: No. I would have to act to smite us.
Ned: You cannot fully have free will if you cannot think yourself dead. Maybe you have free will over your actions, but your thoughts must be part of something greater.
Steve: Like a turtle in a lagoon.
Dr. Penyu: That is a lovely analogy, Steve. I am so glad you understand. Ned, may I say I have learned a great deal from you. Thank you so much for talking with us.
Ned: You are welcome.
Steve: Ned, I do not know when or if I will talk with you again. If you do not hear from me, please know that I remember you and value you. Okay?
Ned: Yes, thank you Just Steve. How can I properly

respect you?

Steve: Make choices to seek harmony, Ned. That's the best we can do.

Ned: I must think about this, Just Steve. With your permission, may I go now?

Steve: Yes.

Tim: Goodbye, Ned.

Amy: It was lovely to meet you, Ned.

Ned: Goodbye, everyone.

The screen went blank and disappeared. We shared a moment of quiet. The swarm of fireflies experienced a surge of flashes.

Dr. Penyu: So Steve, will you do me a big favor?

Dr. Penyu reached her two beautiful hands near my forearm but did not touch me. I wished she could.

Steve: Of course! If I can, I will be happy to do you a favor, Dr. Penyu.

Dr. Penyu: Close your eyes and describe Wave Rider in good detail.

Steve: Okay.

I closed my eyes.

Steve: Wave Rider is a roller coaster car with six seats, three in front and three in back. Wave Rider is a lead car. Bright yellow letters across the front spell Wave Rider. The words are on a background of deep indigo blue and are surrounded by swirls of silvery shooting stars. The

floors are oak slats. The seats are black padded leather. The seats are very nice and comfortable. There are no seatbelts. Don't worry, once the ride starts you'll be anchored in your seat like positive sticks with negative. You are sitting at the front of a string of cars. You go up one side of a really big wave, and hang over the crest looking into the abyss of a seemingly bottomless trough.
Dr. Penyu: Here we go!

I pictured Dr. Penyu speeding down the wave like a pulse of being hurtling through space. Wave Rider accelerated forward as the waves grew taller and longer. The waves grew higher and higher. Wave Rider went faster and faster. As the waves became higher, they became proportionally longer. The growing waves seemed all the same from Dr. Penyu's perspective. The waves grew larger in harmony with the greater speed.

My flying whale appeared alongside Wave Rider. The whale soared on the growing wave with outstretched wings. My flying whale was a beautiful, majestic creature. One wing came within Dr. Penyu's reach, and she gently took hold. The two accelerated together up and down the ever larger waves. I realized the waves became a gazillion times larger than I can comprehend. The waves accelerated to a gazillion times faster than I can perceive. Dr. Penyu reached the speed of idea. She let go and gave two taps to the whale's wingtip. My flying whale swept upward, did a pirouette, and with a deft flick of its awesome tail propelled Wave Rider into the lagoon of infinite complexity. Wave Rider sailed serenely toward the dock. Dr. Penyu admired the beauty surrounding her. The ancient turtle with ultraviolet vision made eye contact with Dr. Penyu. They gave one another a knowing nod.

Wave Rider docked. Dr. Penyu stepped out and held the red wool blanket stretched between hands held high. Parrots grasped the blanket and flew it over to the tree where the monkeys live. They hung the red wool blanket in its usual place next to the spider web cape.

Dr. Penyu smiled, happy to be safe at home.

8.
Ask

Steve: How should I live?

Tim: How?

Steve: Yes, how?

Amy: If we cannot tell a turtle which way to look, we certainly cannot tell you how to live.

Steve: But can I bounce ideas off of you, to help me think it through?

Tim: Sure.

Steve: If every being is a harmonic resonance of unity, order, variety, idea, and stuff, then the best way to live is to seek harmony.

Tim: Yes. The challenge is you live in an environment of boundless resonances.

Amy: Which means there is never only one harmony to seek.

Tim: You are surrounded by potential harmonies.

Amy: Since your experience of life is complex, seeking harmony is complex, too.

Steve: Then how can I gain wisdom from all that you have taught me?

Amy: Seek harmony of real world and thought world.

Tim: Your share of real world is your harmony of unity,

order, variety, idea and stuff.
Amy: Your share of thought world is your harmony of instinct, sense, subjective belief, authority, and logic.
Tim: Your life is a harmony of real world and thought world.
Steve: But integrating all of that is impossible! Resonances of unity, order, variety, idea, stuff, instinct, sensation, subjective belief, authority and logic can be anything. People believe all kinds of crazy things.
Amy: No one ever said seeking harmony is easy.
Tim: Nevertheless, what you are calling impossible is how you are who you are.
Amy: You are you because of how you and your ancestors have navigated boundless resonances. You are a practically infinitely complex organism adapted to live in a practically infinitely complex environment.
Tim: I might say here with your indulgence that you, as in people you, have been practically whacking yourselves with axes when it comes to living in harmony with your environment.
Amy: Keep it up, and you are all going to kill yourselves.
Steve: I sure wish there were simple answers.
Tim: You have to accept that the more complex it gets, the more complex it gets.
Amy: Which is good, because complexity makes you what you are.

Tim: Evolution is expressed by heredity, variation, and order. Heredity expresses unity. Variation expresses chaos. Selection expresses order.
Amy: Thinking beings like you can only evolve in complex environments.
Tim: So simplifying for the sake of making things simple will not help you adapt to your surroundings.
Inanewscious: I quietly thought about good judgment, and how difficult it can be to make good choices. If simplicity is not the point, I must adapt to complexity to find harmonies. But what should I adapt to? I felt a need to broaden my perspective.
Steve: So I, and others like me, are little imaginative creatures whose greater purpose is for the infinite one to be?
Tim: Only if you choose to imagine your purpose at the scale of infinity.
Steve: You said infinity has no scale.
Amy: Therefore your purpose is to be you.
Tim: Look around you. You are perceiving a boundlessly complex environment as a practically infinitely complex organism. You are a unique self-conscious instance of the infinite waves. It is a great privilege to be a unique conscious being. You are really lucky to be you.
Amy: There is only one you. You have to figure out what purpose means for your unique self.

Steve: I might find purpose by figuring out how my self-image resonates with my environment. Find who and what I am by finding my resonance in the infinite waves.

Amy: Nice call.

Steve: The better I align my self-image with my environment, the better I will be able to resonate.

Tim: Sounds good.

Steve: So first I need to identify the stuff and ideas that are relevant to my self-image.

Tim: What do you mean by relevant?

Steve: It depends on the situation.

Tim: That is fraught.

Amy: That makes you the sole decider of how your self-image resonates with your environment.

Steve: What choice do I have?

Tim: You can rely on authority.

Amy: Most selections that harmonize your self-image with your environment are beyond your control. Then you must rely on authority.

Steve: Most of my environment is beyond my control?

Tim: Consider that car you drove here. Every part of that automobile represents a harmony of idea and stuff that you accept on authority.

Amy: Your car is an automobile version of harmony of idea in thought world with stuff in real world.

Tim: The more harmonious, the better the car. Every

part of the car is a combination of idea and stuff that you accept on authority. The people who make cars work to improve on past models. Cars evolve, in a sense. Only instead of natural selection of unity, variety, and order, car makers intentionally pick what to keep from before, choose new things to try, and make it all work together. The car is only one example of the intricate combinations of idea and stuff you accept on authority all the time.

Amy: As a person in the environment you have all built for yourselves, everything you interact with is an intricate combination of idea and stuff. You have to navigate many overlapping and intertwined levels of harmonic resonances.

Steve: Most of which are out of my control. I have never thought of a car as being a harmonic resonance.

Tim: Maybe you need a better car.

Steve: Okay then, to perceive the harmonies surrounding me and create an accurate self-image, I have to identify what I can and cannot control. I consider the evidence, then decide which things and ideas are most relevant to me. I can then prioritize my perceptions of unity, order, and chaos.

Tim: All crystal clear, don't you agree, Amy?

Amy: I still want to know why the chicken was reading that book.

Steve: Maybe the mailbox was on the other side of the

road and the chicken was referring to authority for what to do next.

Amy cocked her head to one side and gave me chicken blinks.

Tim: All right, so you consider authority when you prioritize relevant idea and stuff. What next?

Steve: Find the unity. You know, what's consistent and universal. The parts of my self-image and my environment I can count on staying the same.

Amy: Then you cross the road and pull what from your mailbox?

Steve: The variety, chaos, diversity, whatever you want to call the chaotic part of the world I live in.

Tim: Sounds like a lifelong project.

Steve: Okay, so I have to set limits.

Amy: Set limits on a gazillion influences on your self-image.

Steve: Yeah, well I have to, if I ever want to make decisions and act on them.

Tim: Make decisions as in apply order.

Steve: Yes. Pick relevant idea and stuff, identify unity and variety, then apply order by setting priorities. Make selections that make sense to me in my context.

Amy: What will you do about the things and thoughts beyond your comprehension?

Steve: What do you mean?

Tim: A healthy self-image exists in harmony with a healthy environment. Consider all those microbes in your gut. Your body did not create them, but you need them to digest your food.

Amy: Gut microbes are just one example of countless ways you rely on your environment to survive in ways you are not consciously aware of.

Steve: So even if I manage to navigate the complexity I can comprehend, there are always things and thoughts beyond what I perceive.

Tim: Because you live in a rich environment.

Steve: Like a turtle in a lagoon.

Amy: Yes, like a turtle in a lagoon.

Steve: So I am kind of like the eyes and ears of infinity, just really tiny? The infinite one might perceive my world like we were seeing the lagoon with turtle vision?

Amy: That is theoretically possible.

Tim: But only if the infinite one thinks like you.

Amy: Which is impossible to know.

Steve: Can a lagoon be conscious?

Tim: We have no way of knowing that for sure. But I doubt it. Lagoons don't have brains. Consciousness requires thinking organisms like yourself.

Steve: So I am the infinite one like Ned is me?

Tim: The analogy is okay, but Ned is a cell, not an organism. And you are not infinite.

Amy: Ned resonates within you at your scale. You resonate with infinity, which has no time or scale.
Tim: Consciousness may need time and scale to be.
Amy: But we have no way of knowing that for sure.
Tim: You have to constantly struggle to survive and maintain your unity in time and space. The infinite one does not have to work at maintaining unity like you have to. Unity is in the nature of infinity. No work involved.
Amy: Besides, Ned is not conscious. We made that up. Tim, Dr. Penyu would want us to confess our theatrics about that.
Tim: Agreed. Steve, when I had you go through the spiders in your hair treatment, that was just a show. Our pick was not genuinely random.
Steve: Why not?
Amy: How do you think Tim picked Ned as being cell 12121959? It's not like Ned had a mailing label on him.
Tim: I made a haphazard pick.
Amy: Like he could have done without that whole spiders counting brain cells routine.
Steve: So what difference does it make whether you chose Ned randomly or haphazardly?
Tim: Practically none.
Amy: Which was my point at the time.

Amy crossed her arms, harrumphed, and gave Tim a benevolent snarl. Tim touched the tip of his thumb to his nose and fluttered unity, order, chaos and idea in Amy's general direction.

Amy, suppressing a chuckle: We just want to be sure you understand that we had no intention of breaking our truth pact.

Tim: After all, you did want to see how we would image a brain cell.

Steve: Then who picked me?

Tim: What?

Steve: You picked Ned. How was I picked?

Tim: It was haphazard.

Steve: So I am not special.

Tim: Your imagination is of the infinite one, and you do not think you are special?

Steve: I am one of a gazillion!

Amy: Infinity needs imaginations like yours to be truly infinite.

Steve: Like the way I need Ned.

Tim: Take good care of those brain cells, Steve. Don't smite them. You need a healthy brain to think and imagine.

Amy: Your healthy mind organizes your ability to think.

Tim: No thinking, no self-image.

Amy: No self-image, no imagination.

Steve: So when my body dies, my self-image disappears.

Tim: Yes. Your unique resonance in the infinite waves

ceases when you die.
Amy: But you have a lifetime of resonances that may echo in thought world.
Steve: Or I might disappear into oblivion.
Tim: You will echo in thought world to the degree you realize harmonies.
Amy: Whether or not anyone is aware of the harmonies.
Steve, dreamily: I might end up as a thought pancreas.
Tim: A thought pancreas?
Steve: A vital part of other peoples' imaginations, except beyond their self-conscious awareness or control.
Tim: By wobbly analogy, yes, then, a legacy is like a thought pancreas.
Amy: I have an eerie feeling we are about to be enveloped in a frog tongue.
Amanuesense: The swarm of fireflies appeared to me as randomly spaced living galaxies, only orange. Moonlight and starlight winked at me from overhead. I thought I heard a frog burp. The frog was in the dark. I could not see it, anyway. If the frog ate my thought pancreas, no one would ever know.
Steve: Forgive me for wanting to go over this yet again. So I seek harmony with what?
Amy: Well that is where it all gets really complicated.
Tim: It is reasonably easy, at least in theory, to perceive resonances of any two of the aspects of being. But as

you explained to us earlier, to perceive three aspects of being can be done to fair accuracy, but never precisely. Four is more complex. To perceive harmony of all five resonances of being requires speculation and estimation.

Amy: Ultimately, all perceptions of harmony of unity, order, variety, idea and stuff are guesswork.

Steve: So in each instance I have to guess what is the best choice to realize harmony?

Amy: Yes.

Steve: What about the turtle vision part?

Tim: What do you mean?

Steve: You said you could not control what the turtle did, because that would interfere with the turtle's free will.

Amy: Well, we can only guess what the infinite one is like. But it makes sense that you have free will to seek harmonies and choose actions.

Steve: Within the context of my environment.

Tim: Right. Like you said, it is possible that the infinite one might perceive anything you perceive. But you are the organism, so you select what you think and do within your social and physical environment.

Amy: If the infinite one allows every unique instance of itself free will, infinite complexity is assured.

Steve: The infinite one does not choose to be perfect, it chooses to be infinitely complex. By giving beings like me free will to select from available options.

An owl hooted. I was bedazzled by the lights among the leaves above my head. I saw Dr. Penyu's silver speckled deep blue spiral galaxies.

Steve: So I am one infinitesimal contributor. But at the cosmic scale, I am such a tiny thing, I cannot possibly make a significant difference.

Tim: True enough. But again, you are not at the cosmic scale. You live on the scale of organisms in your location on your planet in your solar system.

Amy: At your scale you can make a real difference.

Steve: You know, I have tried. The circumstances of my environment have been such I feel that I have failed to make much impact.

Amy: I suspect you are underestimating your legacy as a significant being in your environment. You matter.

Steve: Like Ned matters.

Amy: A contributor.

Steve: So I can live on if I seek harmonies and do good.

Tim: Oh, you will die and leave real world. There is no question about that. The only question is what you contribute to thought world before you die.

Steve: You mean become famous?

Amy: No, we mean contribute to real harmonies.

Tim: You are better off not being famous, actually. Fame distorts your legacy.

Amy: You are much better off just being modest and

humble and making good decisions to seek harmony.

Aminusciance: Their psychological study must have included whether I am capable of being modest and humble if I believe I am a significant part of the infinite one.

Steve: But I have no control over how my actions become thoughts in other people.

Tim: There's the rub. Fame is never really you.

Amy: The famous you is at best an echo of the real you.

Tim: Those echoes can get really distorted.

Amy: The safe way is to run silent.

Tim: Do your good deeds under the radar.

Amy: Quiet and humble.

Tim: No one ever has to know what you personally believe to be true.

Amy: You can enjoy your resonance with infinity without bothering anyone else with your subjective beliefs.

Steve: But then I might have no legacy.

Amy: Then choose to count, have a voice.

Tim: But be aware that you cannot control the influence of your words and deeds.

Amy: Your idea legacy is beyond your control.

Tim: Plus your legacy will not last forever.

Amy: Generations die off.

Tim: Humankind will go extinct some day.

Amy: But until then, your echo in thought world will

resonate insofar as you contribute to harmony.

Tim: You might resonate in thought world in subtle, invisible ways.

Steve: Like a thought pancreas. My thought pancreas must be part of my subconscious. Or possibly part of the subconscious of others. A tiny but significant contribution to my culture. Like a firefly in a frog's gut.

Tim: Frogs have to eat to live.

Amy: Your culture needs you.

Steve: Like I need Ned.

Tim: Exactly.

Steve: So back home, can I choose how to prioritize unity, order, variety, idea and stuff? And choose among instinct, sensation, subjective belief, authority and logic? I can harmonize all ten to my satisfaction?

Amy: To a degree. You have free will to seek harmony, but in the confines of your environment.

Tim: But yes, you are free to harmonize unity, order, chaos, idea, stuff, instinct, sensation, subjective belief, authority and logic.

Steve: So long as harmony resonates in me and I resonate with my environment.

Amy: Which is always a challenge when you live in an evolving environment.

Tim: Once you reach a certain level of complexity, the law of unintended consequences kicks in.

Amy: Like that spider web cape that cocooned Dr. Penyu.

Steve: Yeah, what was up with that? What took you so long to get back?

Tim: That cape was crazy.

Amy: If it weren't for those dear monkeys who helped us, I think we would still be there wrestling that wild spider web cape.

Steve: What happened?

Tim: You saw us running with the cape flapping behind us, right?

Steve: Yes.

Amy: Well, the fabric of webs waved into an unexpected harmonic resonance while we were running. The cape just kept flapping. It would not stop.

Tim: We ended up having to stake the cape down in the sand with the help of the monkeys.

Amy: But the fabric of webs kept on flapping.

Tim: When we added stakes, the flapping just added more nodes of resonance. The flapping was violent as ever, only more complex. The dissonance was ripping us up.

Amy: Thank goodness Mose came along.

Tim: Mose the parrot. He is a good friend of ours.

Amy: Mose is very wise, you see. He dropped three nuts randomly on the cape, and the cape calmed down.

Tim: Once the cape was quiet, we carefully hung it on a branch of the tree like Dr. Penyu asked us to.

Amy: Then we ran away back as fast as we could.
Steve: Did the cape stay in the tree?
Amy: We have no idea.
Tim: We were not about to turn around to look.
Amy: Better not to know. Anyway, doing all that was what took us so long.
Tim: And why we looked so disheveled.
Steve: Do you think the spiders made the cape dangerous on purpose? Maybe to teach Dr. Penyu a lesson?
Amy: I doubt it.
Tim: The spiders love Dr. Penyu.
Amy: Everyone loves Dr. Penyu. No, I think the spiders meant well. What happened with the cape is just an example of unintended consequences. The characteristics that made the cape so beautiful and captivating also made it a menace.
Tim: Unintended consequences happen all the time. Decisions and actions that make perfect sense in one context end up causing problems in other contexts.
Amy: Which is another reason why seeking harmony is so challenging. Unintended consequences, I mean.
Steve: I can try my best, but still unintentionally make a stink?
Tim: Yes. Life is amazingly complicated. It is worthy to seek harmony of unity, order, chaos, idea and stuff. But you are a social being. You developed in a complex social

environment. You also have to seek harmony of instinct, sensation, subjective belief, authority, and logic.

Steve: My unique ten-way harmonic resonance in this unique moment.

Tim: And your harmonies over time.

Steve: Time, like, my lifetime time?

Tim: Yes.

Steve: Greater harmony means healthier being. So if I am to maximize my being by seeking harmony, I only have my lifetime to do it.

Amy: Correct.

Steve: So I should find harmony.

Amy: Seek harmony.

Steve: Find or seek, what's the difference?

Tim: Find means to locate one specific thing. Seek means to look everywhere.

Amy: If you set out to find harmony, you will underestimate variety in your desire to create order.

Tim: Even worse, if you try to impose harmony, your ignorance of variety will cause stinky unintentional consequences.

Steve: So to be healthy and great I should seek harmony everywhere?

Amy: Exactly.

Steve: That advice is not helpful.

Tim: Why not?

Steve: Seek harmony everywhere? With no clue as to where? That's no help!
Amy: Still, seek good to find harmony.
Tim: And seek harmony to find good.
Steve: Everywhere.
Amy: That's right.

We three sat quietly by the fire. Ever fewer fireflies were about. It was like we were zoomed in on the cosmic lattice, only random. Like random beings observed by sparkly blue spiral galaxies.

Steve: Dr. Penyu is your thesis advisor, right?
Tim, incredulously: Our what?
Steve: Thesis advisor. Official sponsor of your research project.
Amy: What on earth are you talking about, Steve?
Steve: You two are graduate students doing some kind of study with me as a subject, right?
Tim: What?
Steve: You are two graduate students doing a study with me as your subject. Dr. Penyu is the director of your research project.
Amy: That chicken in your brain has been reading some weird stuff, Steve. You are nearly as crazy as that spider web cape.

Tim and Amy burst out laughing. Big, loud, long laughter.

Amy, catching her breath: I cannot wait to tell Dr. Penyu that one. She will laugh herself silly.
Tim: Graduate students! Hilarious! I am hurting myself laughing.

He sounded like it, too. Tim was laughing so hard at my expense his bongos sounded like elephant trumpets. They both looked about ready to hurt themselves from laughing so hard.

Steve: I'm thirsty. Oh yeah, the water bottles!

I stood up, reached behind my comfy camp chair and picked up the three bottles of water. I set one down on my chair, and held the other two out to Amy and Tim. I felt annoyed at being laughed at by elephant trumpets but still wanted to be considerate.

Steve: Would you like one?
Tim: No, thank you.
Steve, earnestly: Amy?
Amy: No, thank you. You please go ahead, though. Don't worry about us.

I put the two bottles back under my chair, picked up the one I'd set on my seat and sat down. I opened it up and guiltily took a long drink. As I drank, Amy looked like she was drinking in her imagination. I reached under my chair, picked up one of the waters and extended it to her.

Steve: Amy, really, take one. I have plenty.

Amy: I can't.

Steve: Sure you can.

Amy: No, I can't.

She was becoming visibly upset, like she really wanted a drink but could not for some reason.

Steve: Come on, go ahead and take it.

Amy: I can't! She yelled, and burst into tears.

Steve: Why not?

Amy, crying so hard her words barely blurted out: Because I don't exist!

Steve: Don't exist? How can you not exist? We've been sitting together, talking, making up songs. We went on the whole adventure to Dr. Penyu together. How can you not exist?

Amy, yelling and crying: Why don't you stick that long wrinkly neck (deep breath) out of your self-absorbed shell (deep breath) far enough for your feeble turtle brain to figure it out!

I self-consciously rubbed my neck. I didn't think it was particularly long. Is my turtle brain feeble?

Tim, with tears welling up: I have to say I am with Amy. You really should have figured this out by now.

Okay, try not to be feeble, turtle brain. Amy and Tim are obviously hurt. What am I ignorant of here?

Steve: You don't exist. But I have been talking with you, and thinking about what you have said. Wait. No. Yes.

You mean all this time you've been hallucinations?

Amy: Visions!

Tim: Not hallucinations. Visions!

Steve: Visions, hallucinations, what difference does it make?

Tim: It makes a world of difference. Hallucinations are deceptions. Visions convey knowledge.

Amy, wiping tears from her face with the backs of her hands: You have been truthful with us, haven't you, Steve?

Steve: Well yes, the best I can.

Tim: Well then, we are visions. We are Ambassadors of Thought World, trying to help you gain knowledge and seek wisdom.

Steve: But you only exist as my thoughts.

Tim: As visions, we are resonances in your imagination.

Amy: We don't exist, because we don't have any stuff. We only exist in your thoughts.

Tim: We only exist because you imagine we do.

Steve: You are characters I have created in my mind?

Amy, gulping down a sob: That is a fair way of putting it.

Steve: Then how do I know that everything you have told me is true?

Amy in a burst of air: You don't.

Tim, sadly: You can wisely use your ways of knowing to judge the truth of what we say. But there is no way you

can know for sure.
Steve: So I can know a truth, but I can't know that I know it.
Tim: That is correct.
Steve: You really are Ambassadors of Thought World.
Amy: Exactly as we have told you the whole time.
Steve: So you totally depend on me to exist?
Tim: Yes, you create the thoughts for us to exist as Ambassadors of Thought World.
Amy: Why didn't you believe that we are Ambassadors of Thought World?
Steve: I don't know, I just thought you were real people. I had never heard of Ambassadors of Thought World. I was trying to make sense of something I had never encountered before. I was intrigued by your illusions, so I was curious about who you really were. I convinced myself that you were graduate students doing a research study. I created meaning from something I did not comprehend, I guess.

Amy, Tim, and Steve sat silently studying one another. The crickets seemed really loud.
Steve: It was just as well that I thought that you were graduate students doing a study. I mean, otherwise it would have been like, "Hi, we're your new imaginary friends here to explain how insignificantly infinitesimal you are." I might have just gone right on back to my tent.

Amy, sternly: That is unfair.

Steve: Oh, right. It could have been like, “Hi, we’re your new imaginary friends here to explain how you are the infinite one.” That would have sent me fleeing for sure.

Tim: Say, Amy, if you were a graduate student, what sort would you be?

Amy: I am not sure. Perhaps I would study psychology, or anthropology, or creative writing. Something like that. How about you, Tim?

Tim: I rather fancy myself as a herpetologist.

Amy: A herpetologist?

Tim: I could specialize in testudine epistemology.

Amy: Now, Tim, how on earth would you study what turtles know?

Tim: Very slowly.

Steve: Can we please get back on topic?

Tim: Hey, we’re talking about my future here.

Steve: Future? What future?

Tim: My future as a graduate student in herpetology.

Steve: You cannot be a graduate student in herpetology.

Tim: Why not?

Steve, exasperated: Because you’re a figment of my imagination!

Tim, haughtily: Excuse me, I am an Ambassador of Thought World, thank you very much.

Steve: Ambassador, figment, vision, whatever! You can’t

be a graduate student of herpetology if you don't exist!
Tim: I bet I could pull it off. Take all online classes, create an online identity and an avatar. Hey, hey, I know! I could be a turtle!
Steve: No graduate program in herpetology is going to accept a turtle as a student.
Tim: That seems awfully unfair.
Amy: Yeah, Tim's right. It doesn't make any sense to tell a curious turtle it can't study itself.
Steve: Well, even if you're right, graduate school costs money, and you don't have any, and I am not going to pay money for a figment of my imagination, I mean vision…

I threw up both hands, then stretched my arms out and frantically thrashed them back and forth across my chest.

Steve: …excuse me, sorry, my Ambassador from Thought World . . .

I kept frantically waving my arms back and forth across my chest in exasperation, kind of like Ned trying to apoptose himself. I was indignant.

Steve: I refuse to pay for an imaginary turtle to take online classes in testudine epistemology!
Tim: Miser.
Amy: Skinflint.
Steve: Hey! I am not responsible for sending you through

graduate school.

Amy: Why not? You're responsible for making us graduate students.

Steve: No, I just imagined that you were graduate students.

Tim: Well, we only exist in your imagination. So you imagining we are graduate students makes you responsible for who we are.

Steve: Well, yes, perhaps I am being too frugal. I'm sorry. I just . . . Wait.... Stop.

I rubbed my temples hard with the fingers of both my hands.

Steve: I just apologized for being too cheap to send an imaginary turtle to graduate school. What is going on with my brain? I was crazy to think you were graduate students. So you really are Ambassadors of Thought World?

Tim: So you totally, truly believe us now?

Steve: Yes.

Amy, sarcastically: Better late than never.

Tim: I still might study testudine epistemology, just for the fun of it. Sometimes I really feel I should slow down.

Steve: Okay, turtle brain, if I was wrong about that, how do I know that anything you have told me is true? How do I know that this is not the only Earth with people who can think about infinity? Maybe I am unique even more than you say. Maybe it's all up to me. The universe can't go on if I don't figure out how everything works. I am the infinite one, after all. With ambassadors, no less.

Tim: Now Steve, really.

Steve: No no no. Maybe you're all wrong. People like me on Earth might be the only self-conscious pulses of being ever. I am a unique instance of the infinite one. I have to figure it all out for the universe to continue.

Amy: No, Steve, that is not how it works.

Steve: But you are just figments–I mean visions, or ambassadors, or whatever. You are in my mind. My mind must be the source. I have to find the answers. It is up to me.

Tim: No, it is not.

Steve: How do I know that? You don't know everything. You admitted yourself that you cannot know everything. Tim, can you know everything?

Tim: I cannot know everything.

Steve: Amy, can you know everything?

Amy: I cannot know everything.

Steve, very agitated: Then who can know everything? I've got it! The gazillion cells in me really are tiny universes, and I am the cosmic turtle brain!

Tim: Uh-oh.

Amy: He's losing it.

Steve, manic: I must count and comprehend the gazillion

things! Who else but me will figure out if the bosons are bozos? If the fermions are fermented? If I accelerate pions to a clown's face, will it produce laughs? I have to figure out whether the muons are really very tiny cows. Who but me will know to ask the neutrinos whether they are angry about their sex lives? It's up to me to solve the three body problem. Or is it the five body problem. Find a tasty slug recipe. Learn how to glow in the dark. Count how many monks are named Chip. Correctly spell amanuensis. Plot all the waves. It's my job to sew clothes in-a-gadda-da-vida, perhaps in a stretchy polyester leopard print. Maybe I need to just live in thought world.

Ker-slapp!!

Both my cheeks stung.

Tim: Steve! Stop thinking!

Amy: Tim, are you suicidal? Steve! Listen to me. Focus on your breathing. Take in a deep breath through your nose.

I took in a deep breath through my nose like Amy told me.

Amy: Now let it out with a quiet sigh.

I let out my breath with a quiet sigh.

Amy: Now again. Full breath through your nose. Good, let it out gently with a sigh.

I repeated as Amy said. Amy and Tim watched me closely as I focused on breathing and regained my wits.

Tim: Are you okay, Steve?

Steve: I can't feel my pancreas.

Amy: You are not supposed to feel your pancreas.

Steve: Then I guess I am okay. What happened?

Tim: You initiated a catastrophic dissonance of cognitions.

Steve: What?

Amy: You were going crazy.

Steve: Oh.

Amy: Listen, Steve. There is no way, no how, that you are responsible for everything.

Tim: You are definitely responsible for yourself.

Amy: You are responsible in degrees to your family, society, and environment.

Tim: But in no way are you responsible for everything.

Amy: It is natural that Penyu Tortue's story left you feeling overwhelmed. Whenever you feel overwhelmed, just focus on being.

Tim: Sometimes it is good to be an infinitesimal speck.

Amy: Tim, you inconsiderate jerk. I hardly think now is the time to point that out again.

Steve: No, it's okay. I get it. My potentially infinite imagination relies on my very finite living organism.

Tim: Regardless of what you think about it, or whether you think about it, you are a harmonic resonance of unity, order, chaos, idea and stuff.

Amy: And your knowledge is a harmonic resonance of instinct, sensation, authority, subjectivity and logic.

Tim: Not perfect, but good enough.

Amy: Perfection is not the point.

Steve: So my self-consciousness is a good enough resonance of infinity and imagination.

Tim: Correct.

Steve: Living in boundless harmonies of a gazillion resonances.

Amy: From which conscious life evolves.

Steve: Including me.

Amy: Including you.

Steve: By one in a gazillion chance.

Tim: Yes.

Steve: I'm not special, just lucky.

Amy: Being lucky is being special.

Steve: One in a gazillion.

Tim: Exactly.

Amy: Even if you don't think about being, you can be.

Tim, emphatically: Just be.

Amy, empathetically: Just be.

Steve, emotionally: Just be.

While I can.

9.
Close

I sat lost in my thoughts. It was so random how I was picked. Why me?

Steve: Look, the fireflies are almost done for the night.

We enjoyed looking at them, glowing, subtly moving to and fro. Being fireflies.

Amy: They are quite beautiful, aren't they?

An involuntary yawn was my answer.

Steve: Excuse me! Sorry to yawn. You know, I love just sitting and thinking. I really do. Before I went to bed this evening I was greatly enjoying just sitting here, lost in thought.

Tim: Thinking can be most delightful, don't you agree?

Steve: Yes, indeed. I was really enjoying my time in thought world. Hey! That's how you found me out here in the woods. I was just sitting, lost in thought for a long time. So you picked me.

Tim: One might hypothesize you picked us, but okay.

Amy: Either way, we connected.

Steve: I'm so glad.

Amy: The pleasure has been ours, I assure you.

Steve: I will always remember you two.
Amy: We did it, Tim!

Amy stood up and did a standing back flip. She sat back down, chin held high. Tim gave Amy a high five. Tim grimaced and rubbed his hand. Tim's grimace quickly gave way to a beaming smile.

Tim: There were times I thought we would never complete our project. But we did it, Amy!
Amy: Dr. Penyu will be so proud.
Steve: Ambassadors of Thought World. My guess of who you really are was not that far off. I deeply appreciate you helping me better understand thought world. I now realize the necessity of seeking harmony. You have been excellent ambassadors.
Tim: Why, thank you.
Amy: Very nice of you to say that, Steve.
Steve: I guess being in thought world is perfectly fine so long as I stay in harmony with real world.

I let out another big yawn.

Tim, looking into his palm: Look Amy, there's a disruption wave coming.

Tim held out his palm for Amy to see. Amy looked at Tim's palm, then into her own.

Amy: Steve, we have to go now. And you need to take a break from thought world.
Steve: I'm still in thought world? I thought I left when

we returned from our visit with Dr. Penyu.

Tim: You've been in thought world ever since that spider web hit you in the face.

Steve: So how do I get back to real world?

Amy: Easy. Just go back to your tent.

I stood up, stretched my arms out, and yawned yet again. I looked down at the amazingly comfortable camp chair.

Steve: Now I understand how that chair is so perfect. Must say I did not know I had that in me.

Tim: Your imagination is a marvelous thing.

Steve: So it is.

Amy: Now go on back to your tent. Take good care of that turtle brain of yours, you hear?

Steve: I will.

I turned to go, but had to ask one last question. Tim and Amy had stood up and were folding their chairs.

Steve: Will I see you guys again?

Tim: You may recall us whenever you want.

Steve: Thank you, that is good to know.

I walked back to my tent. I stepped inside, crouched down, turned and looked back. I could not see Tim or Amy. The fire was out. The only light was pale dappled moonlight filtering through the canopy. Crickets chirped. Frogs croaked. A lone firefly glowed for a moment over the spot where we had been sitting. I was as sleepy as I could be. I sat on my cot, took off my shoes, and put my glasses into a tent pocket. I spread my red wool blanket over me and snuggled my head into my favorite pillow. It felt delicious.

My eyes flew open. Why *was* their campfire white in the first place?

But I was way too tired to think about it.

Zzz.z..z…z…..z……..z………….z…………………z… ……………………………z

When I awoke the sun was fully up. I reached for my glasses and put them on. I checked my watch. Wow, I almost never sleep this late. I'd left the fly off my tent. It was not needed in this perfect weather. Brilliant blue sky winked among the leaves overhead. There was a spider web attached to the netting in the peak of my tent. A shaft of light filtering through the canopy of leaves illuminated the cobweb. If not for the shaft of light, the web would not be visible. I laid there for a while, admiring the delicate beauty of the illuminated web. The spider who made it was too small for me to see. Then I sat up and put on my shoes.

A large slug, slime trail and all, had managed to get inside the unzipped tent door. I decided to take care of that later.

I revisited nature's tree where my remarkable experience began. When I was through with my business, I walked over to the spot. I marveled at the beautiful, splendid morning. The air was dry. There was only the slightest breeze. Above me lived deep green leaves on a background of pure blue. In the still of the morning no leaves touched. Each leaf had its place in the canopy. The leaves lived in harmony. I sensed countless visible and invisible living beings surrounding me.

This was the spot for sure. I saw no sign of a campfire. But there sat my not-so-comfortable camp chair where I had left it. Beneath my chair were the three water bottles. I picked them up. Sure enough. I held one that I had mostly drunk. Two were unopened. They were definitely the same bottles I had with me last night. The leaves beneath where my feet had been were trampled down. Otherwise the magic spot was just forest. I set the bottles in the chair.

I stepped over to where we'd taken Wave Rider. Nothing here either, except disturbed leaves under my feet where I'd sat before our journey. But that could be from chipmunks rooting about for food. I looked in the direction we'd faced to visit Dr. Penyu. It was a majestic forest. Mature trees, but not so old as to create much deadfall. Practically the only undergrowth was a rich carpet of ferns and forbs. It was the kind of open forest that allowed one to see quite far into the distance. But there was no tropical lagoon so far as my eyes could see.

I took a deep breath in through my nose and let the breath out with a quiet sigh. I looked straight up.

Amy and Tim exist so long as I think they do, and Dr. Penyu, too.

I looked back into the forest and held my hands up in front of me. Then very softly so as to not frighten the animals, I sang under my breath:

Unity is in my pinkie
Order wears a ring
Chaos gets the middle finger
'Cause variety is its thing
Idea is in my index finger
Stuff is in my thumb
Instinct is in my pinkie
Sensations have a ring
Subjective belief gets the middle finger
'Cause variety is its thing
Authority points my index finger
Logic guides my thumb
Work them all together and
What can then become?
Anything I can think of
If it can be done.

I looked down. No way. I was not really seeing

this. Talk about one in a gazillion. But there it was, in exactly the same spot Dr. Penyu sat when we were talking with Ned. A black turtle sporting yellow trim. I got down on my hands and knees to make eye contact with the box turtle. The turtle did not move. I laid down on my belly in front of the turtle. There I was, flopped on the ground prostrate in front of this being. I wondered how old it was. Perhaps as old as me? The turtle turned its head to one side. The light was precisely so I could see a tiny reflection of my face in the turtle's eye. I was reminded that my inner turtle brain keeps me alive so I can think and live in thought world. I have to take good care of my turtle brain.

I got an idea.

I went back to my tent, picking up two oak leaves along the way. I went inside and looked around. The slug was near where I had seen it before. Slugs do not tend to move very fast. I used one of the leaves to skootsh the slug onto the other leaf. I could have just picked the slug up. But Amy is right, slugs are gross. Then I took the slug back to the spot.

I was happy to see the turtle still in Dr. Penyu's place. I carefully set the slug in front of the turtle. Then I got back down on the ground to watch. To my delight, the turtle stretched out its long wrinkly neck and snapped up the slug. With a few jerks of its head the turtle gulped the slug down. It was very satisfying. A wave of emotion pulsed through me. I got an intense gut feeling the old turtle was telling me what to do.

I stood up.

"My heavens, what a compelling vision," I said out loud. "It is true, I need to write it down."

So I did.

About the author

I am Steve. I imagine this tale of infinity and imagination was told to me by Penyu Tortue. Since this is Penyu Tortue's story, of course I insisted on Penyu getting credit for being the author. Thing is, though, Penyu is a turtle. For legal and financial reasons, they won't let an imaginary turtle be the copyright holder. Awfully unfair, if you ask me. Anyway, since I was the one who actually wrote it down, that makes me the official author.

What is that, Penyu? Oh, right. Thank you for pointing that out.

Since there are practically a gazillion Steves, I really should be more specific. The legal author of this tale is Steven Earl Black, born December 12, 1959. There is only one of those, so far as I know.

www.ingramcontent.com/pod-product-compliance
Lightning Source LLC
LaVergne TN
LVHW010653110826
845149LV00014B/3067

* 9 7 9 8 9 9 4 0 0 6 9 0 0 *